Advance P

WHEN LIGHTNIN' STRUCK

"*When Lightnin' Struck* weaves tragedy, bullying, and family secrets into a riveting adventure. A small story with Texas-sized heart!"

—Joyce Moyer Hostetter, author of *Blue*, *Equal*,
and other Bakers Mountain Stories

"A keenly observed and timely story of a Texas boy's discovery of deeply buried family secrets—and of his own humanity."

—Susan Patron, winner of the Newbery Award
for *The Higher Power of Lucky*

"Eleven-and-a-half-year-old James Aaron lives with his grandpa, 'Pappy,' at a diner in Odessa, Texas, in the 1920s. Adventures unfold and suspense builds as family secrets are revealed. James literally holds the key (an amulet) to discovering his true identity in this warm, engaging story that hinges on a little-known period of Jewish history. With vivid food scenes, this is a 'delicious' read!"

—Susan Goldman Rubin, author of *Sing and Shout: The Mighty
Voice of Paul Robeson* and *The Quilts of Gee's Bend*

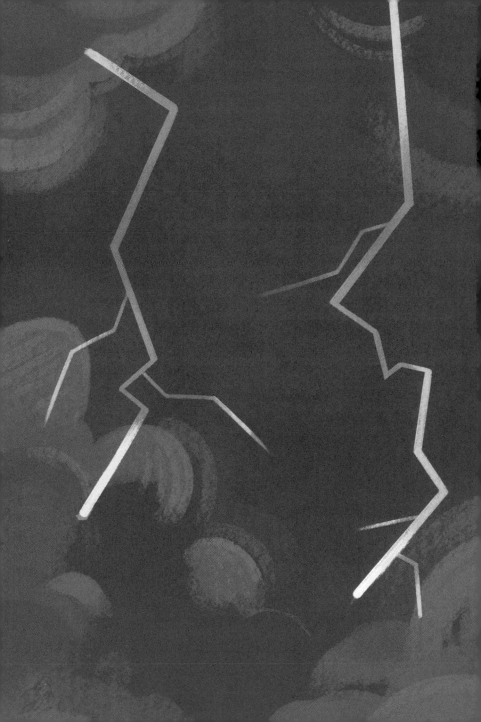

WHEN LIGHTNIN' STRUCK

Betsy R. Rosenthal

KAR-BEN
PUBLISHING

KAR-BEN PUBLISHING®
An imprint of Lerner Publishing Group, Inc.
241 First Avenue North
Minneapolis, MN 55401 USA

Website address: www.karben.com

Cover illustration by Marco Guadalupi.

Main body text set in Bembo Std.
Typeface provided by Monotype Typography

Library of Congress Cataloging-in-Publication Data

Names: Rosenthal, Betsy R., author.
Title: When lightnin' struck / by Betsy R. Rosenthal.
Other titles: When lightning struck
Description: Minneapolis : Kar-Ben, [2022] | Audience: Ages 9–13. | Audience: Grades 4–6. | Summary: In Odessa, Texas, in 1927, eleven-year-old James is dealing with his family's streak of misfortunes, battling a school bully, and searching for his purpose in life when a family secret changes everything. Includes author's note.
Identifiers: LCCN 2021010309 (print) | LCCN 2021010310 (ebook) | ISBN 9781728420523 (lib. bdg.) | ISBN 9781728420530 (pbk.) | ISBN 9781728444253 (eb pdf)
Subjects: CYAC: Family secrets—Fiction. | Jews—United States—Fiction. | Bullies—Fiction. | Family life—Texas—Fiction. | Texas—History—1846-1950—Fiction.
Classification: LCC PZ7.R7194453 Wh 2022 (print) | LCC PZ7.R7194453 (ebook) | DDC [Fic]—dc23

LC record available at https://lccn.loc.gov/2021010309
LC ebook record available at https://lccn.loc.gov/2021010310

Manufactured in the United States of America
1-49146-49296-7/8/2021

For my grandparents—Samuel and Minnie Paul
and Abel and Frieda Rosenthal, immigrants from
Russia and Lithuania all

That which is hateful to you,
do not do to another.

—Hillel

Chapter 1
Fightin' and All

"Your family's got a curse on it!" Virgil hollered at me outside the schoolhouse after Miss Pritchert rang the bell. If anyone was cursed, it was Virgil. He was about as smart as a bag of rocks and as pretty as an old man's toenails.

I balled up my hand in a fist. "The only curse my family has on it is the curse of havin' to live in the same town as your family," I said.

Virgil swiped his greasy black hair away from his face and glared at me outta the dark caves where his eyes were hiding. "You're gonna wish you hadn't said that!" he yelled and popped one on my left cheek. That's when a whole circle of kids started gathering around us.

I clutched my aching cheek and covered my face

so the other kids couldn't see the tears blinding me. Then Virgil pushed me so hard he knocked me down. Along with everyone jeering and yelling stuff, I heard Virgil's sidekick Margaret shouting, "Get him, Virgil!"

Virgil kicked me while I was lying on the hard ground. My cheek smarted and now the back of my head hurt too. Around me it sounded like one giant chant with a mess of different voices until I could make out one voice, deeper than the rest.

"Get up, James. You not listen to them." Lucky for me, it was my best friend, Paul Gudovich. Well, I suppose it was easy to have a best friend when you only got one friend.

Next thing I knew, his strong arms were helping me to my feet. "Come. Let's go from here," he said.

The circle of kids parted around us like the Red Sea. Even though he was only a couple of years older than me, Paul was a giant compared to the rest of us kids, especially me.

But Paul being so tall didn't stop Virgil none from spitting out, "Looky here, it's the dumb Russian giant come to rescue the lightnin' boy midget."

I held my throbbing cheek and sorta leaned on Paul as we walked away from Virgil and his posse. Soon as we were on the path, hidden by the mesquite trees, I sat myself down in the dirt and let go of some of the tears I was holding in.

"Wow, Virgil popped you good this time," Paul said, looking down at me. "What will your grandfather say?"

"Don't worry about Pappy," I said. "He probably won't be sore at me once I tell him that I didn't even throw a punch. You know he don't want me to fight. That's the only reason I didn't squash Virgil."

Paul lifted the corner of his mouth a little. That was the most smiling I ever got from him. "You are sure you would be the one winning such a fight?" he asked. I guess Paul knew me pretty good, even though he hadn't known me for long.

I never heard anybody speak as slowly as Paul did. It was like he was playing a game of hide-and-seek with words inside his head every time he talked. And his accent sure announced to everybody that he wasn't from these parts. I reckoned he'd start sounding like a Texan soon enough, though.

"You walk okay?" he said. "If no, I go bring your grandfather."

I stood up. My legs were working fine. It was my head that was hurting. And my pride even more. "I'm okay," I said. "Let's go."

We followed the path through the mesquite trees. They were about the only things growing in Odessa on account of the dirt was fulla sand and it was so dang dry. It was hard to find any kinda shade anywhere, and even though it was September, I was sweating up a storm.

"You wanna stop on the way and go swimmin' at Perkins' pond?" I asked Paul. I was a whole lot keener on cooling off than having to explain my aching cheek to Pappy.

"Is not good idea. You need something for cheek right now. We get you to your grandfather." I reckoned he was right, so we kept going till we passed Elbert Heath's field and got to Ridgely's, my pappy's diner, which was plumb next door to our house.

"Thanks for helping me out, Paul," I said.

"You be okay?" he asked.

"Sure. See ya tomorrow at school." I gave him a slap on the back. I wished Paul coulda stayed and we coulda worked on our history homework together, but I had to go face Pappy. And I figured he'd be kinda suspicious of Paul. Pappy didn't trust most newcomers—like Paul's family, who came here all the way from Russia not too long ago. Pappy suspected anybody finding their way to our town might have something to hide. Odessa was so far out west in Texas that folks liked to say it wasn't quite the end of the world, but you could see it from here.

The bell tinkled when I opened the diner door, which made it impossible to sneak in. My nose told me Pappy was making Ridgely burgers. He said it was his very own recipe and claimed you couldn't find them anywhere else. He took the ends of the Pullman bread loaves that we couldn't use for sandwiches and soaked them in water and mixed the wet bread ends with some meat. Then he patted the mixture into little hamburgers. The best part was the smell of the frying onions with paprika that he poured over the burgers in the pan.

I expected Pappy would give me a talking-to, but I was sure he'd give me a Ridgely burger too.

"What happened to you, Butch?" he said, looking up from his pan of onions.

"Got in a fight at school. I didn't touch him, Pappy, I swear. I just fought with my words, like you taught me."

He went back to the giant icebox and pulled out a cold, pink ribeye steak. "Here, put this on that cheek and tell me the whole story."

That's one thing I sure liked about Pappy. He'd give you a good listen before he'd tell you what's what.

"I was defendin' the family honor," I said. "Virgil Jackson insulted us. You can't blame a man for not sittin' on his hands while someone's bad-mouthing your family, can you?"

"Maybe not, but I believe your best bet would be to avoid that boy entirely. Virgil Jackson's not worth your time. God put you on this earth for better things, James Ridgely."

"What are those better things, Pappy?"

"I believe each one of us has some kinda purpose on this earth. Your job is to find out what your purpose is, Butch."

I sure wished my abuela—my grandmother—were still alive. I was certain she coulda helped me find my purpose.

Chapter 2
My Sorta Family

While I sat at the counter holding the cold steak on my cheek, Pappy stood at the grill stirring the onions sizzling in the pan.

He eyed me and said, "You sure have seen too dang much at the ripe old age of eleven."

"Eleven and a half," I corrected him.

Pappy wasn't one for smiling, but I thought maybe I caught a hint of a smile. It was hard to tell what Pappy's mouth was up to behind his big, bushy beard and mustache.

"Whatya mean, Pappy?"

"Losing your daddy at such a young age and in such a strange way. Then having your mama behind bars and . . ." Pappy was blinking his eyes a whole lot.

I knew what was gonna come next on the list he

was reciting. He was gonna say that then I lost my abuela. Pappy missed her something awful. They'd been married forever. And 'course he missed my daddy too. The only family Pappy had left was me.

Pappy was right. I had seen a lot, but that didn't mean I understood what I'd seen. I was still looking for answers. Like why my daddy was struck by lightning, outta all the daddies in the world. And why Mama couldn't have kept herself outta trouble, and why Abuela had to go and die when she was the town *curandera* who coulda healed anybody. Anybody excepting my daddy and herself.

"Why was my daddy struck down?" I asked Pappy.

"I don't have a good answer for you. I reckon that it was his time, that the Lord took him for a reason."

"What was the reason, Pappy?"

"I wish I knew," he said. He stroked his beard. "But the Lord's ways are a mystery to me."

I sure wished I knew too. When my daddy died, that musta been the first time I got an awful hollow feeling inside me, like a piece of me had been cut out. And then when Mama got hauled off to jail, that empty feeling where my heart was supposed to be stretched out even more, especially when I'd see mamas and daddies with their kids come into the diner for a Saturday family dinner. When I was living with Abuela and Pappy, some warm feelings finally started filling up that space. But then Abuela went and died, and I got to suffering from the emptiness all over again.

Pappy slid a burger outta the pan, piled it high with fried onions, and handed it to me on a lime-green plate. Whenever I gobbled down a Ridgely burger my mouth was awfully grateful. I stopped holding the steak on my cheek and hoped my cheek didn't look too colorful. I needed my hands for eating. After every last bit of food was gone from my plate, I took the empty dish back to the kitchen. It was 4 p.m. and my shift at Ridgely's Diner was starting. We kept pretty busy in the diner since, as Pappy liked to say, "We're the only game in town." We stayed open till 10 p.m. on weekdays and till the last customer left on Saturdays. Pappy said we were closed on Sunday because Sunday was "God's day."

I took a grease-stained apron off the hook and tied it around my waist. The sink was jammed fulla dirty dishes. That meant lunch business had been good. As I scraped the ketchup and gravy remains off the dishes, I started writing my history essay in my head. Washing dishes was a good time to sort out my thoughts. As soon as I finished scrubbing the pile in the sink, I dried off my hands and pulled my writing pad and pencil outta my knapsack. Before I had to start waiting on the customers, I sat on a stool at one end of the counter and got down on paper what I'd written in my head.

The first customers came in around 5 p.m. It was always the hungry guys from the Santa Rita oil well, the ones who didn't have wives to cook their meals. They took to joking that Pappy was even better than a wife. He was a real good cook, gave the men a hard listen, and didn't yell at them none. I didn't remember my daddy so well anymore, but I did remember Mama doing a whole lotta hollering at him.

The oilmen were sorta like family for me. I never heard them claiming, like other folks did, that we were cursed 'cause of some of the bad luck dumped on us.

Malvern Hill came in first and sat at his usual table. I went over to say howdy and take his order.

"Hey Butch, what's your pappy cookin' tonight back there that looks good?" Malvern asked me. I liked how he called me Butch, just like Pappy did.

"There's nothin' better than a Ridgely burger

in my opinion. But the chili's lookin' awfully good too," I told him.

"You run into a tree?" he asked, reaching up to touch my face with his hand. He was missing a couple of fingers, like a lotta the guys who worked on the oil rig.

"Naw," I said.

"I'm worried about you, Butch," he said. "You keep goin' and gettin' yourself pounded. Was it Virgil Jackson again?"

"Yup," I said. I didn't want to go into it with Malvern, but he wasn't any fonder of Virgil than I was—especially after last Halloween, when Virgil overturned Malvern's outhouse while Malvern was in there doing his business.

"Are you fightin' back at all?"

"I fight pretty good with my words. Pappy won't abide by me usin' my fists."

Malvern just nodded. He understood without me saying so that Pappy didn't want people thinking I had trouble controlling myself. Truth was, I was kinda glad Pappy forbade me from fighting. I was scrawny for my age, and fighting back probably wouldn't have done me much good. I was keen on keeping my nose on my face, right where it belonged.

And if I did start brawling, then maybe I'd end up in trouble with the law like Mama had.

Pappy once told me that God deals each of us a set of cards and we've got to show him what kinda players we are. He said Mama wasn't dealt a full deck. But I was pretty certain she did get a full deck, and somewhere along the way her cards got too soggy from the drink.

I didn't get to see her too much anymore, only when Pappy agreed to take me to visit her in jail. And he wasn't too keen on taking me. He claimed it was 'cause it wasn't so easy for him to leave the diner. But I was pretty sure the real reason was that he didn't think my being around Mama was too good for me.

Whenever we did drive out to see her, it was usually only after a whole lotta pestering on my part. Jail or no jail, she was still my mama, and when she was feeling okay, we'd have ourselves good talks. But I never could talk to her the way I could talk to Abuela. Until last school year, that is, when Abuela went and died and left me and Pappy on our own.

Chapter 3
My Favorite Person

It'd been about six months since I last laid eyes on my abuela. When I first went to live with her and Pappy after Mama got hauled off to jail, Abuela seemed fine and kept real busy doing her usual, mixing up herbs and the like for people who needed healing, and traveling to their houses to treat them. Ever since I was little, she'd been taking me with her when she went hunting for special plants and herbs for her cures. She even let me tag along sometimes when she called on folks who needed healing. After Mama got hauled off to jail and I went to live with Abuela and Pappy, Abuela brought me along a lot more and took to explaining to me what she was doing to treat her patients.

"James Aaron Ridgely, you're smarter than

a hooty owl," she'd say with her Mexican accent, looking me right in the eye and holding my cheeks between her warm hands. "You catch on to everything so quickly."

But then Abuela got real sick. She took to her bed more and more, and after a while she was too weak to leave it. One day, Pappy told me her end was nearing, so I stayed by her all day. He even let me skip school.

Abuela was lying in her bed with her head propped up on pillows. It was the first time Pappy had left her side that day. The room smelled funny, like a mixture of garlic and rubbing alcohol. On the bed table and bureau there were a bunch of *velas*—little candles—that I'd seen Abuela use in her healing practice. She said the burning candles were for getting rid of the bad spirits in the room. She told me to light them. I was all for doing whatever needed doing to banish any spirits that were making my abuela sick. In my mind they were downright evil.

"Come here, James," Abuela whispered.

I could tell it took her a whole lotta effort just to push out those words. I scooted my chair up next to her and leaned my face real close to hers. "I'm right here, Abuela."

She took ahold of my hand. I always loved the feel and smell of her hands, like warm tortillas. But they weren't warm this time. She smoothed out my palm with her wrinkled fingers. Then she slipped a small, roundish metal thing that looked like a coin into my hand and squeezed it shut.

"*Mi nieto*, keep this always and do not show anyone," she said in a shaky voice that I could barely hear. "One day you will understand what it means."

"What is it, Abuela?" I asked. I wanted to open my hand to look at it more closely, but she kept her hand wrapped around mine.

Her eyes were fixed on me, but she didn't seem like she was seeing me, almost like she was looking right through me. "And please do not forget my teachings," she whispered. "I am ready to leave this world, but my spirit will still be with you always."

Her eyes fluttered closed, but she kept ahold of my hand, the same hand that held the thing she gave me. I shook her arm real lightly and said, "You can't leave me, Abuela. Tell me what I can do to heal you. There must be somethin'."

Then in a voice so hushed I had to put my ear right up to her lips to hear, she said, "Bring your pappy now."

"Okay. I'll be right back, Abuela," I said.

Just as soon as I left to fetch Pappy, I ran smack into him in the hallway outside their bedroom. "She told me to get you," I said and turned to go back into the room.

He stopped me, setting his hand on my shoulder. "I need to go in there by myself." He went inside and shut the door.

I stayed in the hall. While I was standing there, curiosity grabbed ahold of me. I needed to take a close look at the metal thing Abuela had given me. I opened my hand slowly, as if it was gonna jump out and bite me. It wasn't much bigger than a buffalo nickel, but instead of being smooth all around, the outer edges were jagged with little peaks and valleys, making it look kinda fancy. I was sorely tempted to rush in and ask Abuela to explain what it was, but I wasn't about to cross Pappy. I was still busy ogling it when I heard the door creaking open, so I closed up my hand real quick.

Pappy finally came out. Our eyes met and he shook his head. Then his whole face crumpled. "She's gone," he said, choking on his words.

"No!" I cried. I tried to go into their bedroom, but Pappy wouldn't let me. Instead, I ran to my room, slammed the door, and fell face down on my bed. I couldn't stop the sobs from bursting outta me like a wild bronco fresh outta the gate. Not my abuela. She was the one always healing everybody. Running eggs over my body and making me drink awful-tasting teas whenever I was feeling poorly. Why couldn't she have healed herself that way? It wasn't fair. Why was God taking everybody away from me?

I sat up and swiped at my tears with one hand, while still holding tight with the other to what Abuela had put in my palm. I was afraid that if I let go of it, I'd be letting go of her. I wanted to keep her with me as long as I could. But I finally opened my hand to look at the coin-like thing some more, to try to puzzle out what it was. There was a tiny loop at the top—so's you could put it on a chain and wear it around your neck, I figured. I never saw Abuela wearing it, though.

It seemed like it was made outta silver, but silver that was sorely in need of some polishing. On one side was some sorta writing. But not English, that was for sure. The other side had a raised picture over the smooth silver of what looked like an extra-wide candleholder. I sat on my bed for a long time, staring at it and rubbing my fingers over it. It was the last thing besides my hand that Abuela had touched 'fore she passed. I needed to find a safe place for it. So I hid it in the bottom of my bureau drawer under my waist union suits. I wasn't gonna tell a soul about it, not even Pappy. Abuela gave it to me in secret, and I planned to keep it a secret.

***

Back in the spring, we buried my abuela in the cemetery outside of town. I'll never forget the date she died on account of it was April 1, 1927. I even prayed that her dying wasn't real, that it was nothing but some awful April Fool's joke that God was playing on us. But nobody answered that prayer.

A lotta folks came up to me at her funeral to tell me stories about how they had gone to see Abuela after Dr. Johnson, the town doc, couldn't help them none with their sicknesses. And how Abuela cured them with her curandera remedies when nobody else could. 'Course Malvern was there, his eyes fulla tears the whole time. Some of the other oil rig guys showed up too, and patted me on the head. Fanny Crawford from my class came along with her daddy, the reverend, who performed the service. Fanny showing up and giving me a comforting hug and telling me how sad she was for me gave me a warm feeling. I sorely wished Mama coulda been at the funeral, but she was stuck in jail.

That empty space I felt inside me when they put Mama in jail got a whole lot bigger when Abuela died. It didn't help that Pappy wasn't keen on taking me to see Abuela in the cemetery. Even though it'd been more than half a year, I kept on talking to her. I missed her something awful. "Abuela, what is this coin-like thing you gave me?" I asked her in my head. "And what's this writing on it?" It musta been real important, maybe even dangerous, for her to make me keep it secret. More than anything else, I kept asking her to help me find my purpose.

Not long after she was gone, I said to Pappy, "I wish I could have a talk with Abuela. I got things to ask her."

"She might not be around to answer your questions, but she does still talk to you, James," Pappy said. "And she'll keep on guiding you. Whenever you do the right thing, that's your abuela speakin' to you. You'll carry her inside you always."

I thought I understood what Pappy was getting at 'cause right before she died, Abuela did say that even though she was departing this world, her spirit would stay with me.

Since I couldn't have a real live talk with Abuela anymore, I felt a need to talk to my mama. When Mama was feeling okay, she could be real loving. If something was bothering me, she'd give me a right good listen and know just what to say to make me feel a whole lot better. People just didn't see that side of her, the side she showed me. Probably 'cause most of the time when they were around Mama, her good side was drowned out by the bootleg.

I sure wished Abuela were here to cure my mama of what ailed her. But since she wasn't, I hoped that some of Abuela's healing talents rubbed off on me so I could try to help Mama on my own.

Chapter 4
What Happened to Mama

Folks in town said Mama was always "troubled" and that she didn't get too good of a start on this earth on account of her mama died giving birth to her. And her daddy was a drinker who went and got himself killed in a brawl with some fellas he was working with, laying the railroad tracks. I heard Pappy say once that considering how she grew up, it was no wonder my mama suffered from the besetting sin.

I knew some folks blamed her for not having been a good enough wife, and they gossiped about her not being a good mama to me. But she sure as pie didn't throw that lightning bolt at my daddy. Still, Pappy got so angry at Mama sometimes that I could tell he wished that lightning bolt had struck her instead of his only child. Folks said Mama was in a real bad way after Daddy died. I guess I was too little when that happened to pay much heed.

Some things I remember clear as glass, though. Mama started throwing loud parties on Sundays, inviting over the kinda folks who had no use for Prohibition, the kinda folks who knew just where to get moonshine from the bootleggers. They carried on at our house till the wee hours. In the mornings, I'd find Mama asleep on the sofa or the living room rug. I'd have to make my own breakfast 'fore I headed off to school. Most of the time, I'd just dump some Grape-Nuts in a bowl and drown them in cold milk.

Sometimes, after my grandparents found out about one of Mama's parties, they'd storm over to our house, steaming mad. One time, the day after one of those parties, I was just getting home from school when I overheard Pappy say to Mama in a voice just a hair shy of a holler: "What in tarnation are you thinkin', havin' those good-for-nothin' boozehounds over? What kinda example are you settin' for your son?"

From the front porch, I heard Mama moaning and Pappy still giving her what for. "You're darn lucky that the sheriff hasn't thrown you in jail for violatin' Prohibition. One of these times, you're gonna get yourself in trouble with the law. Then who'll take care of James?"

Hearing that, I stayed on the porch for a while and held on to my belly, which was giving me some pain. I already had no daddy. Pappy's words made me start fretting about losing my mama too.

I forced myself to go into the house. When I did, I saw Mama lying on the sofa, her face sorta greenish and her mustardy-colored hair matted down. She was pressing a wet cloth on her forehead. She did that a lot on the days after one of her wild parties.

Abuela caught sight of me walking in, and she laid her hand on Pappy's arm. "Settle down, Jeb," she said. "James is home." In her other hand, she was holding her medicine sack.

"Lucinda, I brought some things over to help you. To help you get rid of the evil spirits that are residing in you," Abuela said real gently, like she was talking to a child.

"I'm not gonna let you practice your hokum on me," Mama said.

"At least let me give you something for your *jaqueca*—your headache," Abuela said.

"Well, I wouldn't object none if you've got somethin' to take away this pounding in my head," Mama mumbled. Her eyes were watering. From the pain, I reckon.

Abuela went into the kitchen for a while and came back with a steaming cup of hot chocolate. She had Mama sit up and drink it and then told her to lie back down. Then she pulled a piece of flat cracker bread outta her sack and placed it on Mama's forehead. But soon as Mama saw Abuela taking an egg outta her sack, she snapped, "That's enough, Marlena. Don't go wavin' that egg over my body. I appreciate the help, but you and Jeb best be on your way now."

Before they left, Abuela wrapped me in her arms. She felt like a warm blanket around me. "If you or your mama need anything, come fetch me," she whispered. "I'll see you soon, nieto." She kissed the top of my head.

"If I hear you've been throwing more of your drinkin' parties, I'm comin' for my grandson and takin' him to live with us," Pappy warned Mama on their way out.

But Mama threw another party anyway, the very next Sunday. Like always, I hid in my room and read. I was making my way through *The Call of the Wild* and as usual got so caught up in the book that I plumb forgot what was going on around me. I found myself shivering cold in Alaska with the sled dogs, so I climbed into bed and pulled the quilt over me and kept reading. My eyes started drooping on account of it was so late at night. I closed the book and pulled the covers over my head to block out the noise from the living room, but I couldn't sleep a wink on account of all the loud, off-key singing. Then came the shouting. When I heard the sound of breaking glass, I had to see for myself what was going on, so I got up and went out into the hallway.

It was Mama doing the hollering. "Get y'all's hands off me!" she screamed, while she kicked at the sheriff's deputy who was pinning her hands behind her back and putting handcuffs on her. He dragged her to the front door.

"Let go 'a me!" Mama screamed. "I need to take care of my boy." She was shaking her head around so much that her long hair was whipping her in the face.

I ran over to where Mama was struggling with Deputy Fry. "Let go of my mama!" I yelled. "Don't take her away."

Mama looked at me and stopped kicking and squirming. But Deputy Fry kept ahold of her.

"James, go back to your room," she slurred. "We'll work this out."

I didn't know what else to do, so I went into my room and shut the door. Then the shouting started up again. I clamped my hands over my ears to block it out. That did about as much good as a chicken's wings 'cause a second later I heard someone banging on my bedroom door. I didn't budge, but inside my belly there was a whole lotta twisting and turning. I didn't want to know who was coming for me.

Sheriff Hammer opened my door. "You okay, James?" he said. His face was all red and sweaty.

"I'm all right, but what about my mama?"

"I've warned your mama one too many times about breakin' the law, havin' alcohol here," he said. "She's gone too far this time, James. We're takin' her to the jailhouse."

"Please don't take her, Sheriff," I said. "She didn't hurt nobody."

"I'm afraid she nearly did, son," the sheriff said. "She got herself all worked up and threw a bottle at the wall that barely missed Stetson Dennies's head."

"But you can't take her away," I said. "Who's gonna take care of me?"

Chapter 5
My New Home

Pappy and Abuela fetched me that night. It wasn't so long ago that Pappy had threatened to take me from there. I wondered if he knew it was gonna happen so soon. Abuela told me to gather my clothes and my books, and she bundled everything up in a bedsheet.

"Come, nieto." She took my hand and led me away from the only home I'd ever known in my whole nearly eleven years on this earth.

Pappy was kicking at the empty bottles of moonshine littering the yard. "Disgusting," he grumbled. "What kinda mother raises a child like this? We shoulda taken you home with us a long time ago."

Abuela patted his arm and whispered something in his ear. Strands of her shiny black and gray hair had escaped from the hair clip.

She bent down and lifted my chin, looking at me with her sad brown eyes. "It will be okay, James," she said. "You will come live with us while your mama gets the help she needs."

I wondered if Pappy and Abuela knew what folks said about Mama. I'd heard plenty from Virgil Jackson and Margaret Bossco and other kids at school. They said that most people wouldn't dare set foot in our house since my daddy died. That only the wrong sorta people came over. That Mama had too much of the devil in her. That she wasn't right in the head, like she had some kinda sickness.

At my grandparents' house, my daddy's old room became my room. I kept my clothes in his bureau, and I slept in his bed. Since I was only around five when he got struck by lightning and died, most of the time I didn't remember him so good. The older I got, the more he disappeared from my head. It was like my daddy got caught in a Texas sandstorm and I couldn't barely see him through all that dust. All I could make out was a fuzzy outline of him.

But staying in his room, I sorta felt him there, and it helped some of my memories come outta hiding. Pictures of me and Daddy together popped into my head. I saw him lifting me up high and setting me on his shoulders so I could touch the clouds. I saw him bringing me a slice of fresh-outta-the-oven apple pie from Ridgely's, where he worked with Pappy. I saw him rubbing ointment on my chest when I had a bad cough. And with me living in Daddy's old room, I think maybe Abuela and Pappy felt like they had their son back. Sometimes, Abuela even called me James Joshua by mistake. That was my daddy's name.

"I want you to do some healing on your mama, James," Abuela told me one day.

"But remember how ornery Mama got when you tried to do a *limpia* on her?" I reminded Abuela. A limpia was something I had seen Abuela do a whole bunch of times on her patients. She'd sweep over the ailing person's body with an egg and then break the egg into water and read the patterns it formed. The patterns told her what was wrong with the person.

"Don't give up on your mama, James Aaron," Abuela had said. "You being her son, maybe she'll let you try to heal her."

"Even if she'd let me, I can't do a limpia on her on account of I don't know how to read the egg patterns," I said.

Abuela said she could teach me, but she got sick pretty soon after I moved in. She couldn't stay on her feet too good and took to her bed a lot, so she sent me out more and more to gather the herbs she used for healing her patients. I knew what to look for on account of she'd showed me which ones helped with which ailments and which ones only made a person sicker.

But Abuela passed on before I ever had a chance to try out any healing on Mama.

Chapter 6
Too Much Quiet

A month or so after Abuela passed, I was ready to see what I could do to help Mama. So I gathered up some rosemary, basil, and rue twigs and tied them together in a bundle with red string like Abuela had taught me.

"Can you take me to see Mama tomorrow?" I asked Pappy.

"Things are awful busy in the diner, James. Why don't we skip this week?" he said. It was always busy in the diner. He wasn't ever too keen on taking me to see my mama. Most of the time, he ended up agreeing to take me, but only after I asked and I asked, probably just to get me to quit pestering him.

"Please, Pappy—I really need to see her," I said.

Pappy stroked his beard and looked hard at me. "Well, it's gonna have to be a real short visit then," he said. "You best get yourself home from school tomorrow without any dillydallyin'."

The next day, I hightailed it home from school and tossed the healing herbs I had collected into one of Abuela's sacks before Pappy and I headed for the jailhouse.

When we were getting in the truck, Pappy pointed to the sack I was carrying. "Whatya got there, Butch?"

"Some special herbs. I'm fixin' to try some healing on Mama like Abuela wanted me to."

"I don't know, Butch. The sheriff's deputy might think you're plannin' to launch an attack with those herbs to bust your mama outta jail."

I mighta detected the shadow of a smile peeking outta Pappy's bushy mustache and beard.

When we got to the jailhouse, Pappy came in with me like he always did. Walking into that place was like going from daylight to dusk. No matter if it was blinding bright outside, it was always gray inside.

Deputy Fry came over and took my sack. He was a tall guy, thin as a fiddle string, and had a long neck with pink splotches on it.

"Whatya got in here?" he asked, peeking inside. "You're not supposed to be bringin' stuff into the jail, kid."

"Just some herbs to help my mama feel better," I said. "Can I please keep the sack with me, sir? I promise I'm not tryin' to make trouble."

Deputy Fry handed me back the sack. "Okay, but no funny business. I'll be keepin' my eye on you."

Soon as Mama sat down at the wobbly visiting table, Pappy said a real quick howdy to her and told me he'd be back to get me in half an hour. Then he skedaddled, like he a-feared if he stayed any longer he'd catch the plague. I could tell he had a mind not to be around Mama any longer than he had to.

There were a coupla guys in the other cell making a racket.

"Shut your traps," Deputy Fry snarled. "Let's have us a little peace and quiet."

Usually nobody was in the other cell, but when we did come across guys locked up there, especially the ones causing a disturbance, Pappy'd tell me they were "unsavory characters" and that I shouldn't pay them any heed. But even after these guys quieted down, my nose was having a hard time ignoring them. They smelled like they hadn't been near a washbasin in a month of Sundays. And the whole jailhouse had a stale, vomity stench. Someone as pretty as Mama sure didn't belong in a dirty, stinky place like that.

I sat down across from Mama. "How are you today, Mama?"

She didn't answer. She just sat in silence and stared at the floor like I wasn't there at all. On some visits, she'd get that old lively look I loved. When she'd see me walk in, the sparks would nearly pop outta her green eyes, reminding me of the sparklers we waved on Independence Day.

But not this time. She didn't ask me if I was washing behind my ears and minding my p's and q's, or how things were going at the diner, or if I had a girlfriend. She looked so sad, like she'd been eating sorrow by the spoonful. I babbled on about nothing special, trying to fill up the silence with some sound. I held Mama's hand so she would know for certain I was still her boy. Then I took the bundle of herbs outta my sack and waved it over her body. I kept waving it while I recited a coupla Hail Marys, like what I thought Abuela woulda done. Maybe I didn't do it right 'cause Mama didn't even look up.

Before our visit was over, just like every other time, I asked her, "You need anything, Mama?"

And like always when she was feeling poorly, she answered in a scratchy voice, "I need your daddy back." At least she'd said something, even though she still didn't lift her eyes.

'Course I couldn't give my daddy back to her. I hardly even had any memories left of him to hand her. I didn't see the lightning strike him, so all I knew about how he died was what I heard tell. Folks said that when it happened, he was at a farm outside of town, buying some vegetables for the diner, and there wasn't even a drop of rain to give him a warning about the storm coming. Townsfolk said my abuela tried everything she could to keep him alive, but nothing worked.

I guessed Mama still missed Daddy something fierce, which was kinda strange on account of most of what I remembered was her hollering at him about one thing or another. Maybe Mama just needed somebody to shout at in that ole jailhouse.

"Ready to go, Butch?" Pappy was back to fetch me. "Did you try your healin' on her?" he asked as we climbed into his truck.

"Yup, and I don't think the herbs did a lick of

good. Mama's havin' one of her silent spells," I said. "Is she gonna get outta that jail soon? It's not helpin' her any to be there."

"Don't rightly know, Butch. Not until she's better, I suspect."

I missed Mama, but truth was—and I felt guilty thinking it—I was getting used to the quiet life Pappy and I had. I didn't miss those raucous parties of Mama's none. But sometimes I had a hankering for some company and big-family kinda noise. I could sure get my share of that at Paul's house, where there was a crowd of people living and everybody was all talking at once in their own language. And after sitting with Mama through one of her bad days, I coulda used a friend. So I planned to head over to Paul's right after church on Sunday.

Chapter 7
God's Day

Sunday finally came, thank the Lord. I wasn't thanking the Lord on account of I was such a believer or anything. I was grateful for Sundays because I didn't have to go to school or work at the diner then. And Sunday meant I'd be going over to Paul's after church. The only thing that made attending church every Sunday halfway bearable was the fact that Fanny Crawford, the reverend's daughter, was there too. She was easy enough to spot with her curly hair the color of ripe lemons.

Fanny was different from the other kids. She didn't look at me funny on account of what happened to my daddy or because of my mama's troubles landing her in jail. With her big round eyes the color of the blue in a crayon box, she looked straight into mine. And she wasn't one bit shy about saying howdy to me no matter who was looking on. Soon as Pappy and I sat ourselves down in a pew, I caught her eye. She gave me a wide smile that showed off the dimple in one of her cheeks. It made my insides feel as good as when I was eating my favorite berry pie. But even with Fanny there, I still couldn't wait for church services to end so I could use Sunday for what Mama said Sundays were made for—fun.

While I sat in First Christian with Pappy, I started daydreaming, like I had a habit of doing. I thought about how Abuela used to take me to her Catholic church over on 5th and Washington. I wouldn't let on to Pappy, but the honest truth is I preferred the way the prayers sounded over there. They sounded more ancient. That was probably on account of all the chanting in Latin. It was sorta like visiting at Paul's house when everyone was babbling in what I reckoned was Russian. In Abuela's church, I felt like I was an explorer traveling to a far-off place, discovering some new land.

I musta been tapping my knee like I do sometimes when I'm stuck somewhere I don't want to be 'cause Pappy reached over and stilled my jumpy hand with his. I knew I was supposed to pay attention and all, but I couldn't help myself. All those prayers and hymns didn't hold my interest none. I sure hoped all my not paying attention wasn't gonna land me in the wrong place after I died, instead of up there with the angels and Abuela and my daddy.

I shook my head, trying to clear out the stuff that was keeping me from concentrating on the reverend's words.

"We are well loved by the Father," Reverend Crawford said in that deep voice of his. "We pray for His guidance—to know His purposes and plans for you and me."

Why was everybody talking about us having a purpose all of a sudden? I had no idea why God put me on this earth. And with my abuela being gone, I couldn't think of anybody else who'd be able to help me figure that out. I deserved a good kick in the shins for not asking her while I had a chance. On top of that one elephant-sized question, I had a whole mess of other questions that I shoulda asked, like about her family, about why she didn't say much about her people, and about how she came to be a healer.

Smack-dab in the middle of my wandering thoughts, Pappy elbowed me.

"Pay attention, James," he whispered. Everybody around me was singing a hymn. I guess my closed mouth gave me away. I looked over at Fanny, who appeared to be singing with all her heart, her body swaying to the music. I joined in, but it wasn't a minute before I got lost in my thoughts again and misplaced the words to the hymn.

Lucky for me those thoughts carried me straight through the rest of the boring church service. I sang the closing hymn with a full voice. I took a last look at Fanny, who saw me and waved. Then I darn near dragged Pappy from the church. Back at home, I stuffed some sandwiches and cakes in a knapsack and went to fetch Paul from his house. He was a good enough friend that I was fixing to take him to my special place.

Chapter 8
My Special Place

I got to Paul's house lickety-split, on account of it wasn't too far from us. His house was real wide—what folks called a double shotgun. If you took the house me and Pappy lived in and pasted it to the house next door to us, that was about the size of Paul's house. His family sure needed the extra space, since they had a lot more people living there than we did in ours.

Inside, everyone in his house was talking or shouting at once, and of course I didn't understand a word they were saying. Their language sounded nothing like church Latin and more like they were clearing gobs of phlegm from their throats. There was a fresh-baked, mouthwatering smell in the house. Paul's *bubby*—that's what he called his grandma—was always cooking when I came by. I figured she pretty much lived in their kitchen. Soon as I walked in the door, she darn near pushed me into a seat at their long pinewood table that took up about half of their living room. Then she went back to the kitchen. I could hear Paul's mama and his aunt Yetta in there, sounding like they were barking orders at Paul's sister, Frieda, who was only six years old. They were hollering something like, "*Gay avek!*"

"What's that mean?" I asked Paul.

"Means *go away*," he said.

His stepfather, Samuel, and his uncle Ruvin were sitting in the two armchairs, hunched over a chessboard, pointing at the pieces and having an earsplitting argument. They both had long, messy beards. The only difference was, Samuel's was black and Ruvin had a long white beard like Noah in my old picture-book Bible. And they always wore black bowler hats, even inside the house. The two of them stopped their arguing long enough to greet me with nods and then went right back to it.

Paul's bubby came back and slid me a plate of some gooey apple stuff wrapped in flaky dough. If heaven had a smell, I was sure it would resemble the scent of Bubby's apple pastry. She sat down right across from me, resting her chin in her hand and keeping her eyes fixed on me without saying a word. She had a hint of a mustache on her upper lip. I knew she was waiting for me to taste the pastry, but I felt kinda funny with her staring so hard at me. Instead of picking up my fork, I started squirming in my chair. Paul came to my rescue. After he said something to his bubby, she got up and went into the kitchen and came back with a plate of the apple stuff for Paul.

"Is strudel. Is very excellent. You try it," Paul said with his mouth full.

I took a tiny bite, not being positive that it would taste as good as it smelled. It was warm and sweet and melted in my mouth.

"Mmm, mmm, this sure is tasty," I said. "The only other things I ever tasted this good were the *bunuelos* that my abuela always used to make right around Christmastime."

"Bun . . . what?" Paul asked.

"Bunuelos. They're these fried dough balls sprinkled with cinnamon sugar. I guess instead of makin' the star-shaped sugar cookies that the kids bring to our teacher for Christmas, she made bunuelos. But not for Christmas exactly, just somewhere around that time."

You'd think I hadn't had anything to eat in weeks the way I shoveled in Bubby's pastry and scraped off the last of the apple filling sticking to my plate. I woulda picked up the plate and used my tongue to lap up any leftover bits, but Pappy woulda had my hide if he ever got wind of me not minding my manners like that.

Bubby nodded at me, and when she got up to take my plate, she patted my head. I'd never seen her smile, but I got the idea that she was real pleased with me, considering I'd gobbled up every morsel on my plate. She said something to me in their language that sounded like, "*Es gezunterheyt, boychik.*"

"What's she saying?" I asked Paul.

"She like you, James, and she say it is to your good health."

"Thank you, ma'am," I said and gave her my biggest smile. Then I turned to Paul. "You ready to go?"

We were heading out the door when Paul's mama called from the kitchen, "*Zay gut*, Pinkus!"

"What's that mean?" I asked. "You in trouble? Your mama always sounds so serious."

"No, she is not angry with me. You might not believe, but my *muter* used to be happy and laughing very much before . . . but she could not smuggle her sense of humor outta Ukraine. She left it there."

"So, what's she hollerin', then?" I asked. "Somethin' about the color pink?"

"We go hike now," Paul said and slipped his knapsack over his shoulders.

But as soon as he closed the front door, I asked him again, "What's a pinkus?"

"Is my name," he said.

"Your name's not Paul?"

"When we first come to this country, to Galveston, kids in school are calling me Pinkus Stinkus, so Mama let me have American name. Paul sound more American, no?"

"Yeah, I guess so," I said. "And Paul's a good Christian name too. Paul was an apostle in the Bible."

Paul started shifting his weight from one leg to the other, like he did when he was bothered by something. "I did not know this when I chose name," he said.

"I bet Virgil woulda had a good ole time with your real name. He definitely woulda called you Pinkus Stinkus."

"Where will we hike today?" Paul asked. He was already taking his giant strides, and I was struggling to keep up with him.

"I got a special place I wanna take you to," I said.

"What is it?" He raised his dark brows like two question marks.

"Wait till you see."

We walked in silence for a while. My head needed a little rest after all the noise in his house and the loud preaching at church in the morning. We had some miles to go to our destination. But it wasn't rough hiking seeing as the whole area was just plains, as flat as a dollar bill. And it was bone dry that day, like it was most of the time. We didn't pass much that was alive excepting some tufts of dry grass and a horned toad here and there. I knew some of the boys from school came around there hunting rattlesnakes for their skins, so we had to keep vigilant and watch out for rattlers.

Paul's not a big talker, so he probably coulda gone on keeping quiet the whole hike. I was getting bored, so after a while, I broke the silence. "How come you don't have to go to church, Paul?"

"You not have our kinda church here," he said, as slow as usual. It was that slow talking and his leaving out some words and mixing up others that made the kids in school think Paul didn't know which end was up. That and the fact that he was bigger, a whole lot taller, and older than everybody else in our grade school. He coulda been in high school, but the teachers told him his English needed some improving first.

"Where you came from, did your preacher give his sermons in Russian?" I asked. "Hey, can you teach me some Russian? We could talk about Virgil Jackson and the other good-for-nothin's at school, and they wouldn't know what we were sayin'."

"No, I cannot."

Before I could ask him why not, he crawled inside himself like a snail disappearing in his shell. Pappy had told me it was sometimes best to leave a man be with his private thoughts. "That's his property, and you got to respect the *No Trespassing* sign across his forehead," Pappy had said.

Right then, Paul took a wrong step and went tumbling into a buffalo wallow. Luckily, he landed on his behind. Not so luckily for him, the wallow still had some water in it from the summer storm we'd had not too long before.

"You okay?" I asked. I laughed at him a little as I stepped down into the muddy hole to help him up.

"Yes, but pants are not very okay. Mama will not be happy. What is this hole?"

"The holes around here are buffalo wallows. Used to be buffalo all over Odessa," I said.

"What is buffalo?"

"Animals that look like big old cows that roamed in these parts. The Apache used to hunt 'em for their hides and their meat."

Paul raised his eyebrows. "Apache?"

"They're the people that lived in these parts in the beginning," I said.

"And what means wallows?"

"Well, the buffalo pawed and rolled around in the dirt, tryin' to get them ticks and fleas off . . ."

"What is ticks and fleas?"

"Hold your horses. I didn't even finish explainin' wallows yet." Paul and I climbed outta the hole. My shoes looked as muddy as his pants. Pappy was gonna give me what for if I walked into the house with that mud.

"Like I was startin' to say, the buffalo rolled around in the dirt to get the bitin' bugs off, and they made these holes. The holes filled up with water whenever it rained, and the buffalo drank from 'em and played in 'em."

I waved my hand over the area around us. "Keep your eyes peeled for buffalo bones. Pappy told me he used to find 'em around here all the time."

Paul's eyes started darting in every direction.

We hiked another coupla miles, yapping about this and that and scouring the ground for buffalo bones. Paul picked up a big rock, black as coal and shiny and shaped kinda like a bear.

"From where you think this rock comes?" Paul asked.

"I'll show you where it's from," I said. "We just have a short ways to go still."

Paul put the rock in his knapsack, and we kept walking.

Suddenly Paul stopped dead in his tracks. His dark eyes went wide, and he pointed at the ground about twenty-five yards ahead of us. "What is that?!" he asked.

"Our destination. The special place I told you about. Come on."

I pulled Paul with me right up to the rim. We stood shoulder to shoulder staring down into the gigantic, hollowed-out opening in the ground. It was hundreds of feet wide and looked like it coulda been a soup bowl for the giant in *Jack and the Beanstalk*.

"*Vaunderlikh!*" Paul said. It musta been his word for *Wow!* His eyes were near bulging outta his head.

"That there is a crater made by a meteorite that crashed to the ground somethin' like sixty-three thousand years ago," I said. "Or maybe Martians or some other space aliens threw it down at us, dependin' on who you wanna believe."

"What is meteorite?" Paul asked.

"Meteorites are things that come from way up there in the stars, and they fall to earth with no warnin'," I explained. "I heard that this here crater is at least five hundred feet wide from rim to rim."

"What is rim?" he asked.

Man oh man, he had more questions than our teacher Miss Pritchert put on our history tests. "You wanna hear the story about how people discovered what happened here or not?"

"I do, yes," Paul said and picked up a rock and tossed it deep into the crater.

"So, there was this local fella who had a strange-lookin' rock sittin' on his desk that he was usin' as a paperweight. And don't ask me what a paperweight is."

"Yes sir, no more questions," Paul said, and clapped his hand over his mouth.

"One day, a geologist—that's a rock expert—came into town and saw that paperweight and knew from the minute he laid eyes on it that it was no ordinary rock."

Paul unbuckled his knapsack and pulled out the rock he'd found. "Is this what paperweight looked like?"

"I reckon so," I said. "That geologist fella figured out it was a piece of a meteorite. I guess you also got yourself a piece. Good thing you found it 'fore it found you. One time a fallin' meteorite landed smack-dab in somebody's backyard. Eighteen-pounder!"

"That would not feel good to fall on my head," Paul said.

"Makes me think a giant is tossin' rocks at us from someplace high up. And probably laughin' about it too," I said.

"Why we not climb down?" Paul asked.

It was kinda steep from the rim to the bottom, so we slid most of the way down on our behinds. If my overalls weren't dirty cnough before, they sure were after the sliding. The whole bottom of the crater was fulla dust and silt.

"The first time I saw this crater was when Pappy brought me here after my daddy got struck by lightnin'. He said he wanted to show me how great the forces of nature are and how tiny we are before them.

At first, I didn't really get what he meant 'cause I was so little. I guess it even scared me a little, but I reckon it was his way of tryin' to help me understand why my daddy was done in by nature."

Now that I was older, being in this place helped me cotton on to how small we humans were in the universe, how I was barely a freckle on the earth's body. I could think big thoughts there. The meteor crater was all the church I needed.

Paul and I sat in the dirt at the bottom of the crater. I stretched my arms out wide and said, "Bet you never seen anything like this where you came from."

"We have meteorites in my town, Odessa," Paul said.

"What're you talkin' about? This is Odessa." I figured there was some language confusion setting in.

"Maybe I not tell you this before, but the town where I am from was also called Odessa. And we, too, have what you call meteorites that fall there. But I never saw one making so big a hole like this."

"Holy pretzel! Are you pullin' my leg?" I asked.

"I'm not pulling on you," Paul said.

"You really came from a place called Odessa? And you ended up in this Odessa?" Paul was sure fulla surprises sometimes.

"Yes, our home in Ukraine was in Odessa," Paul said.

"So, which Odessa came first, ya figure?" I asked.

"I think your Texas Odessa is named after my Odessa because railroad workers here said this place remind them of their home in Ukraine. Is why Ruvin, my *feter*—my uncle—he came here, to Texas Odessa. He was looking for place like home." Paul brushed his hand over the dirt, and his next words sounded like they got stuck in his throat. "Same name, but better place for our family than Ukraine Odessa, he hopes."

"Well, I, for one, am grateful that somebody named our town Odessa. It sure beats the name it had before—Milepost 296! If it was still called Milepost 296, your uncle never woulda come here, and I never woulda met you," I told him. "What was so bad about your Odessa that y'all left it, anyhow?"

Paul shook his head, but he didn't say a word. It was real clear to me that there was a *No Trespassing* sign posted on his forehead. Paul was like Pappy in that way. He didn't like talking none about what made him sad. He preferred keeping his sadness buried inside.

Without our voices, it was silent in the crater.

Until we heard *kee-eeeee-ar, ke-eeeee-ar.* We both looked up to the sky and saw a hawk circling overhead. It made me think of my abuela. One time when she and I were out gathering some healing herbs, we spied a hawk flying above us.

"Look, mi nieto—it is a messenger from the angels," she'd said, pointing up. "When you see a hawk, it means it is time to spread your wings and fly higher than ever before, so you can see *todo el mundo*—all the world."

"But I can't fly, Abuela," I'd said.

She'd tapped her heart. "Your spirit can fly. And just as the hawk has the sharpest eyesight of all the birds, you, too, will see everything." Then she had wrapped her arm around my shoulder, and we'd stood watching the hawk together for a long time. I wasn't sure I'd gotten her meaning. I thought maybe it had to do with me needing to open my eyes wider, or something like that.

I got so lost in remembering that time that I plumb forgot where I was for a minute. Till Paul nudged me and said, "Where did you go, James?"

"Just thinkin' about my abuela. I wish you coulda met her. You woulda liked her, and she woulda liked you."

Paul nodded and said, "I wish, too."

I felt the air getting cooler and noticed the daylight was disappearing inside the crater. "We better head back. Pappy's gonna have my hide if I don't get home before dark."

"And Mama will hit me on head with a teakettle if I get home in dark," Paul said.

"For real?" I asked. His family was loud and his mama seemed kinda tough, but they didn't strike me as the hitting type.

"No, I just say that. She only ever *patsh* me on *tuchas* when I was little." He pointed to his behind.

We hightailed it outta there, trying to beat the sun before it set. I shoulda known we couldn't make it. We had too far to hike still. The last few miles we were stumbling around in the dark. We got a little spooked hearing the hooty owls calling.

Suddenly, there was rustling coming from the brush. I stopped dead in my tracks and grabbed Paul's arm. "You hear that?" I said. I was afraid it was a rattler. We ran a little to get clear of the rustling sound. We couldn't see much in front of us on account of our only light came from the slice-of-melon moon. I took a step and found no ground under my foot, just air.

"Darn!" I yelled from the muddy buffalo wallow I had tumbled into.

"Now you are the klutz." Paul laughed and pulled me out.

I was so wet with mud that I sloshed the rest of the way home.

"Explain yourself, James," Pappy said soon as I walked into the house, all muddy and cold.

"Me and Paul, we just hiked too far. I'm real sorry, Pappy," I said. "I didn't mean to worry you none." If there was one thing I had learned, it was that telling the truth usually got me outta trouble quicker than telling a tall tale.

"You're not going anywhere after church next Sunday," Pappy said, wagging his bony finger right close to my face. "Maybe that'll remind you to follow the rules around here. Sometimes I fear you've got some of your mama's wildness in you."

The next Sunday was sure gonna be a boring day.

Chapter 9
History Lesson

At school the next day, I didn't rightly know why, but Miss Pritchert decided that Paul was gonna give the class a history lesson. Paul always had his head stuck in a book, so maybe she figured he had a lotta interesting stuff stored in his brain that he'd learned from his reading.

I guessed Miss Pritchert knew what she was doing. Pappy said she was a mighty fine teacher. When the folks in town called her an old maid, he defended her, saying she was married to her teaching. Pappy also said there was nothing wrong with her looks, so she could surely find a husband if she wanted one. She had a deep dimple in her chin, a small nose as pointy as my pencil after I sharpened it, and brown hair that she kept in a real tight bun at the back of her head. It looked so dang tight it must've felt like someone was yanking on her hair all day long. I saw her at the Piggly Wiggly more than once, and I hardly recognized her with her shiny brown hair waterfalling around her shoulders.

To begin the lesson, Miss Pritchert asked Paul to stand up in the front of the class and tell us about Russia. It seemed to me that was akin to demanding someone stand up and tell everything there was to know about the United States of America. Where would you start?

"Afterward, y'all can ask him any questions you want to about his country," Miss Pritchert said.

Paul started scratching his head and staring at the back wall of the classroom. I could tell he didn't like being put on the spot like that one bit. It meant he was gonna have to air out some of the stuff he kept tucked away.

"I am from Ukraine. Was part of Russia, but now is part of Soviet Union. In Ukraine, we have not weather like Texas. We have so much snow and so cold winter that if the head is not covered outside, you will grow icicles in hair."

Some of the kids chuckled when he said that.

"Paul, could you tell the class a little bit about the government in Russia?" Miss Pritchert asked.

Paul started shifting back and forth from one long leg to the other.

"Again, I am from Ukraine, but I can tell you about Russia government. Like in this country, they have revolution. They get rid of tsar."

"What's a tsar?" Fiona blurted out.

"Is like king. He lived in palace with much servants, beautiful clothes, paintings, and jewels. But at same time, many people have very hard life there. People not even have enough food for eating."

"So, now do you have a president like we do? Someone like our Silent Cal?" asked Chester.

"No. The people do not choose leader like here in America. The name of leader there is Josef Stalin. He is very cruel. The soldiers keep him in power."

"You seem very knowledgeable about Russian history and the government, Paul," Miss Pritchert said.

"Yeah, but not about how to talk right," Virgil piped in.

"That's enough, Virgil," Miss Pritchert said sharply. I sure was glad our teacher didn't let Virgil get away with every mean comment that shot outta his mouth.

Fanny raised her hand. "Why did your family come to Odessa, Paul?" she asked. I turned my head to sneak a smile at her.

"My uncle come to Odessa first. You see, in Ukraine we lived in city also called Odessa. The land here is flat like in my Odessa where we grew much wheat. Texas Odessa remind my uncle of home. Was hard life in Ukraine, and he hear that there is much opportunity in Texas for better life. I think this is true."

"Thank you, Paul, for sharing a bit of your background," Miss Pritchert said. "I'm sure the class would like to hear more about your country another day."

"Wait! Say something in Russian," Margaret blurted out.

"*Poshla K'chiortu*," Paul said.

"What's that mean?" Margaret asked.

"Have a good day," Paul translated, but he gave me a look that told me that wasn't what he really said. Later, when I asked him about it, he told me it meant, "Go to devil!" Hearing that just made me like him even more.

***

60

When Paul and I started walking home after school, Virgil and his regular posse of three—Margaret, Elmer, and Earl—followed us. Elmer and Earl were brothers, but you couldn't tell from looking at them. One was short and squat, and the other was skinny as a bean pole and a head taller than his brother. And they didn't have enough sense between them to spit downwind.

Sweat was collecting on my brow, partly because it was a scorcher of a day, but also partly on account of I could see we were being ambushed. Margaret came right up to Paul and stood on her tippy-toes, trying to get a look at the top of his head. She reached her fingers up to touch his scalp and asked, "Whatya do with your horns?"

Paul swatted her hand away like it was a pesky fly. I didn't know what in tarnation Margaret was talking about.

"My daddy says that you people have horns, just like the devil," she said. Margaret's daddy musta had a screw loose was all I could figure.

Paul turned his back on her and started walking away.

But Virgil caught up to him and poked him in the arm. "Hey, big dummy, when you gonna learn how to talk right?"

"When you learn how to add two plus two," I told Virgil.

He glared at me. "Ain't nobody talkin' to you, lightnin' boy! Whatya really come here for anyway, Russia boy? For zis and zat?" Virgil was spraying spit while he laughed.

We kept walking, but Virgil continued jabbing his finger at both of us nonstop. Paul coulda licked him easy if it had just been Virgil, but we were outnumbered. And anyhow, I guessed Paul had had enough trouble where he came from. He wasn't looking for more.

Virgil and his gang finally stopped the taunting when Malvern showed up on the path and scowled at them. They trotted back toward the schoolhouse, yukking it up like they were watching a Laurel and Hardy routine. I said see ya later to Paul, who went off toward his house, and Malvern and I headed for the diner.

Malvern wasn't very tall, but as Pappy liked to say, he was "as solid as a brick building." And what Malvern was lacking in hair on the top of his head, he sure made up for with his hairy eyebrows. They formed one bushy brown line above his eyes like a caterpillar running across.

"Why aren't you at the oil rig?" I asked. Malvern usually didn't come in to eat at the diner until quitting time, about 5 p.m. or so.

"Takin' a late lunch break and then goin' back," he said. "Looks like I ran into you and your friend at a good time. Virgil botherin' you again? You want me to say somethin' to his daddy?"

That's what I liked about Malvern. He always offered to help out. He had no family of his own, so I guess we were the closest thing he had.

"No, thanks. I can handle it. He'll just get madder if he finds out you talked to his daddy."

Malvern and I walked along silent for a spell until he started singing one of his oil songs:

> *A driller's life, I know, is filled*
> *With crosses and with care*
> *But beyond the grave, he's richer*
> *Than any millionaire.*

There wasn't much to look at on the way to the diner except a family of lizards sunning themselves on a rock. The day had been awfully warm even though it was fall already. I reckoned the critters were out in plain view by then only 'cause it was late enough in the day that it was starting to cool a bit. Some bright orange flowers caught my eye, and I yanked a few off the bush.

Malvern stopped singing. "You remind me of your grandmother. She was always pickin' leaves from the plants around here, always on the lookout for ingredients for her healin' remedies. What're you gonna do with those, Butch?"

"I don't rightly know, but I remember Abuela tellin' me how she had people chew on the roots as a cure for somethin' called pleurisy—a problem in the lungs."

"Your grandmother was somethin' special, all right," Malvern said. His eyes looked watery. "Did I ever tell you about the time she healed me right up?"

Even though I'd heard the story a million times before, I let him tell me again.

"Once when I was burnin' up with fever, your grandmother brought me soup every single day, put cool cloths on my head, and ran some herbs over me. And she made me drink this awful-tastin' stuff that got me right back on my feet. Said it was elderberry flower and willow. I think I made myself get well just to avoid havin' to drink any more of that concoction."

I wondered if my missing her was ever gonna go away. I was still carrying around a whole mess of questions about her and some of the things she used to do. And I didn't have much luck getting answers from Pappy. I got an empty feeling in my gut, knowing that I wasn't gonna get a chance to ask her about anything ever again.

"Hey, maybe you inherited your abuela's healin' skills," Malvern said. "She once told me that she learned about the plants from her grandmother, who learned from her grandmother and so on, going way back to Spain."

"I never heard nothin' about Abuela's people comin' from Spain," I said. "All's I know is that Abuela came here from Mexico. Isn't that why people called her a *Tejano*?"

"I guess that's right. She was from Mexico, and her family crossed the Rio Grande to escape the civil war over there. And when they got here, her father worked on building the railroad, right along with your pappy when he was a young man."

A picture of Abuela came into my head from that very first week when I went to live with her and Pappy. The sun had been in the middle of setting and I'd been hungry, so I'd gone into the kitchen. I saw her waving her hands over two lit candles that she kept in little clay pots on our eating table. And she was whispering some kinda mumbo jumbo. I was standing behind her, so I couldn't hear it very well, but I thought maybe it was one of those blessings she used in her healing practice.

"Whatya doin', Abuela?" I had asked.

"*¡Dio mio!*" she had cried and jumped a little.

I musta startled her. She had suddenly stopped reciting whatever it was she'd been reciting and had given me one of those worried looks like she used to give me whenever she was feeling my forehead for a fever.

"Oh, mi nieto, I didn't know you were here," she had said. "I was . . . just saying a little prayer. Now that you're living here, you'll see me do this often. Let's just keep it between us, okay?" I didn't know why she said that, but I kinda liked having a secret with her.

The burning candles didn't surprise me none on account of when Mama and I used to go over to Abuela and Pappy's house for dinner sometimes at the end of the school week, there were always lit candles on the table. I didn't even think to ask her why she lit those candles. The best part of going over there for dinner, besides Abuela's tamales, was when she brought out a deck of playing cards and we got to play Hearts by candlelight. My whole family played cards over there when I was real little: me, Daddy, Mama, and Abuela. Pappy wasn't usually with us on account of he was working at Ridgely's, feeding the Friday night dinner crowd.

"Where'd you go, Butch?" Malvern asked. "You got real quiet."

"Thinkin' about my abuela," I said.

"I bet you miss her a whole lot, huh?"

"Yeah." I started making a list in my head of questions I wanted to ask Pappy about my abuela. The hard part was gonna be finding the right time to get Pappy talking. While I was busy wandering around in my thoughts again, suddenly Malvern shoved me off the path.

"Get outta the way!" he yelled. And he kept pushing me farther from the path, making me fall right into a pear cactus.

"For land's sake!" I said, getting to my feet. "Whatya do that for?"

Malvern pointed back to the path. A coiled snake was hissing something fierce.

"That there is a rattler." Malvern's voice was

shaking like Jell-O and his face was white as a cloud. "If that guy got his venom in us, we'd be in real trouble, especially without your abuela to give us some kinda antidote."

With that angry snake blocking the path, we had to go the long way around to get to Ridgely's. We brushed past some mesquite shrubs, and their thorns just added to the scratches I'd already collected from the prickly pear. Soon as we walked in, Pappy saw me go over to the kitchen sink and start cleaning the blood from my arms and hands.

"How'd you get them scratches?" he asked.

"Ran into some prickly pear and mesquite when Malvern saved me from a rattler we met up with." Come to think of it, that was the second snake Malvern had rescued me from that day, if you count Virgil.

Malvern winked at me and took his usual seat at the counter.

"Sit down, Butch," Pappy said. He boiled some water and slid a cup of steaming hot cocoa over to me. Since Malvern was our only customer at that hour, Pappy got started preparing his dinner. While Pappy was tending to Malvern's burger sizzling away on the grill, I decided to try again to get Pappy talking 'cause it seemed like his mouth worked a whole lot better when his hands were busy too.

"Pappy, you never told me I got family way, way back from Spain," I said.

The creases around Pappy's eyes got deeper. "Malvern, I appreciate you rescuin' the boy from the rattler, but what've you been fillin' his head with?"

"Nothin' much, Jeb," Malvern said. "Marlena once told me her ancestors came from Spain. That's all I shared with the boy."

Pappy turned to me. "Ancient history, James. Nothing worth knowin' about." He put out the *No Trespassing* sign across his forehead, and I knew no more words would be escaping from his mouth. He disappeared into the kitchen to finish cooking up Malvern's order. And, as usual, I was left to puzzle over stuff on my own.

***

Late that afternoon, I ran over to our house and dug out the coin-like thing from Abuela that I kept hidden in my bureau drawer, buried under my clothes. I took to thinking of it as my good-luck charm, since it did look like some kinda charm. Maybe Abuela gave it to me to protect me. From what, I didn't rightly know.

I rubbed the charm hard between my thumb and my index finger. I could feel the raised outline of the candlestick picture on it. I didn't know what I was expecting to happen when I ran my fingers over it, but nothing did. I'll admit it—I was hoping a genie would pop out and grant me three wishes, like in that Aladdin story I'd read a long time ago. I knew what my wishes woulda been. The first two woulda been for my daddy and Abuela to both be alive again. But Pappy had taught me that there was no coming back—that those who died wouldn't want to come back anyhow on account of they were enjoying the peacefulness of heaven. That left only my third wish—for Mama to come home. I planned to wear Pappy down with my pestering to get him to take me to visit her the next day so maybe I could see about getting that wish to come true.

Chapter 10
Visitin' Mama, Then Pappy Meetin' Paul

While we were waiting for Deputy Fry to bring
Mama out from her cell, I held my nose like I usually
did on account of how bad it smelled in that place.
Worrying about what kinda mood Mama was gonna
be in made the inside of my stomach feel wrung out,
like when Pappy squeezed all the water outta the
dishrags before he used them again.

Soon as she came out, Pappy said, "Hello, Lucinda
May. How are you feelin'?" He stayed standing,
ready to make a quick getaway.

He asked her the same question every time we
visited, and I don't rightly think he cared much to
hear her answer. It was clear as a cloudless sky that
Pappy didn't think too fondly of Mama.

"Happy to see my boy is what I am, Jeb," she

answered, sounding like anybody else's mama. And when she looked at me, giving me one of her big, wide smiles with all her pearly whites showing, I knew she was having one of her good days.

"Well then, I'll leave you two to your chat. James, I'll be back to fetch you in a half-hour's time. We gotta get back to town before dinnertime, remember." Pappy never did stay for more than two minutes.

Mama and I sat at the battered table in the little visiting area, with Deputy Fry leaning against the wall, watching, of course. First thing I noticed was how Mama's hair was reaching down almost to her elbows. I guessed the sheriff hadn't let her get her hands on a pair of scissors to give herself a trim. Maybe he was worried that she'd use them to cut her way outta jail somehow. At least her hair looked clean and shiny as a brand-new copper penny. The sheriff musta let her give it a good washing. And that day, her eyes were greener than anything growing in Odessa, including the agave plants. It was the natural color of Mama's eyes when she was thinking clearly and staying far away from the drink. But being cooped up inside that jailhouse for so long had pulled all the color outta her cheeks.

"Your pappy been good to you?" Mama asked.

"'Course."

"That don't surprise me none. I know you're in good hands. Your pappy loves you somethin' fierce." Then with her hand that was colder than the privy seat in winter, Mama grabbed ahold of my hand and started asking me the usual questions: "Are you washin' behind your ears? You mindin' your pappy and helpin' him out at the diner? Are you still the smartest boy in school?"

Then she asked my least favorite kinda question.

"You sweet on any of the girls in your class?" Her eyes were laughing. "Why is your face turnin' the color of ladybugs, James Aaron?"

Even if I was kinda sorta sweet on Fanny Crawford, I sure wasn't gonna let my mama know about that. I was more than happy to steer our talk in a different direction.

"I got somethin' to ask you about, Mama," I said.

"What's on your mind, James? You got furrows in your brow deeper than a well."

"Well, it's about Daddy," I said. "I don't remember him so good anymore. He was pretty strong, wasn't he? And tall?"

"Your father was as tall as a mountain and as strong

as they come—on the outside. But softer than a pillow on the inside, mind you. You just keep a picture of him, of what you do remember of him, in your head. And if your picture starts fading, just look in the mirror. Then you'll know exactly what he looked like. You're just a smaller version of him, that's all."

Mama had that twinkle in her eyes like she got when the world was making sense to her. So I figured it was a good time to ask her about something else that'd been eating at me.

"Mama, do ya think our family's cursed? I mean on account of what happened to my daddy and . . ."

"And the fact that your mama's in jail?" She ran her fingers through her long hair. "Who's sayin' we're cursed?"

"Some of the kids at school. Virgil Jackson for one."

"Let me tell you somethin' about Virgil. His daddy's a good-for-nothin' dewdropper with a real mean temper, and ever since that boy's mama picked up and left, Leroy Jackson's been takin' out his anger on Virgil. No doubt that boy's got an urge to pick on somebody 'cause Lord knows he's havin' a rough time of it at home. Lightnin' strikes that house every day for Virgil."

"But are we cursed, Mama?" I asked again.

"I don't believe in curses. We had some bad breaks, your father and me, but that don't mean we're cursed. In fact, if anything, we're blessed. We got you, didn't we?"

We kept yakking. It was mostly Mama telling me stories about my daddy. But in no time she said, "Now give your mama a kiss goodbye. I see your pappy coming."

***

On Monday after school, I invited Paul to the diner for supper. I didn't bother asking Pappy's permission first because if I had, he'd'a said no on account of he doesn't cotton to new people or outsiders easily. He liked to brag about how he could trace the Ridgelys all the way back to the *Mayflower*, and he acted real suspicious of people from outside Texas, especially foreigners. It never made a whole lotta sense to me considering he married my abuela, who came from Mexico. Didn't that make her a foreigner? But then again, Pappy didn't have much use for most of the locals neither, especially the ones who believed our family was cursed. Pappy told me not to pay them any heed, saying they had more than enough space in their heads for collecting foolish ideas.

"Pappy, this here is Paul Gudovich, my friend from school. And Paul, this is Pappy." I wanted to start things off on the right foot by practicing my manners.

"Is nice to meet you, Mr. Ridgely." Paul nodded at Pappy and tried forcing his mouth into a smile. Paul knew how to be polite, but smiling didn't come too easily to him. Just like his mama.

There was no hint of a smile on Pappy's face either. 'Course with Pappy's mess of a gray beard, it wasn't so easy to see what his lips were doing. He had that disapproving look in his eyes, though. I could tell Pappy was making Paul nervous because Paul took to scratching his thigh.

"Hope you don't mind, Pappy. I invited Paul to supper. Could you please make us a coupla Ridgely burgers?"

Turning to Paul, I said, "You never tasted anythin' so mouthwaterin' good as one of Pappy's Ridgely burgers."

I was holding my breath, hoping Pappy would see his way to inviting Paul to take a seat at the counter. Instead, he asked in that gruff, disapproving voice he used sometimes, "Where are you from, boy?" His arms were folded tightly across his chest, and his eyes were giving Paul the once-over.

"We live on Marland Street." Paul was speaking even slower than usual. I reckoned he was trying something fierce not to make any mistakes with his English.

"I didn't mean what street do you live on," Pappy said. "I mean where do your people hail from?"

"You'll never believe this, Pappy," I piped in. "Paul's family comes from another city called Odessa. But Paul's Odessa's in a country called Ukraine. And his uncle settled in our Odessa on account of it reminded him of his home. Whatya think of that, Pappy?"

"Not much," he said with a snort. "So, what was wrong with your own Odessa that made your people wanna leave the place?" Pappy's eyes bored into Paul like an oilman drilling deep into the ground.

"We had no freedom in my Odessa," Paul said. "We could not go where we wanted. We could not study in regular schools. We could not work in many jobs. It was not safe. Soldiers attacked us. Here in America, we have freedom." Paul's eyes turned a shade darker, and there was a fierceness in them that I hadn't seen before.

Pappy seemed to understand something. His eyes softened, and he uncrossed his arms. "I see," he said. He pointed to the stools at the counter. "Have a seat."

***

Pappy stood at the grill behind the counter, frying up our burgers. "What brought you to Texas of all places?" he asked Paul. "And how long ago did y'all come?"

"Uncle Ruvin was here first. He came because of the name Odessa and because he think there is much work here with the railroad and the oil. I came with stepfather, mother, and sister to Galveston first. Then to Odessa in time for school to begin."

"I see. So, you and James met in school, I take it?"

"We just met in September, on the very first day of school, Pappy," I said. I couldn't ever remember hearing Pappy asking somebody so many questions. And it didn't seem to bother Paul one bit. The questions finally stopped when Pappy slid the plates of food over to us. I guess Pappy didn't want to make Paul talk with his mouth full.

Paul gobbled up his Ridgely burger. He licked every finger clean. "Thank you very much, Mr.

Ridgely. The food was very excellent." Paul sounded like he'd been practicing that line.

Then he brought his dish back into the kitchen and washed it himself.

"See ya at school tomorrow," I said as Paul walked out the door.

I figured that after Paul left, Pappy would give me a good tongue-lashing for not asking permission first before inviting him over. I was too chicken to even look Pappy in the eye when I headed to the kitchen to help out. I was waiting for Pappy to let me have it, but it was quiet enough in the diner that I could hear the onions sizzling. Pappy looked up from his frying pan and said, "Nice boy. Don't mind if you bring him around again."

Holy cow! Pappy was plumb fulla surprises.

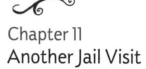

Chapter 11
Another Jail Visit

The same week that Paul came to the diner, I had
a strong hankering to see my mama. I thought if
she was okay again like at our last visit, I'd be able
to ask her some of the questions that were crowding my head. First off, after seeing how interested
Pappy was in learning about Paul's family, I wanted
to ask Mama why Pappy wouldn't talk much about
our own family and especially about my abuela.
It seemed like every time I asked him something about her, he put up his *No Trespassing* sign.
I thought maybe I'd ask Mama about the charm
too, even though Abuela had told me not to show it
to anyone. Mama wasn't gonna go blabbing about
it. There was nobody in the jailhouse for her to talk
to anyhow.

Like always, I badgered Pappy till he agreed to take me.

"Tomorrow, Butch," he said. "But we'll have to leave straight away after school and before the dinner crowd, so get yourself over here soon as the school bell rings. No dawdlin'."

I tried to keep my head down after school let out, hoping Virgil wouldn't notice me. It seemed like his favorite hobby was picking on me. Paul and I started down the path away from school together.

"You want come to my house today?" Paul asked.

"Can't. Goin' to visit my mama," I said.

Suddenly, I got shoved from behind and landed on my hands and knees in the dirt.

Virgil looked down at me. "Hey lightnin' boy, where you off to in such a hurry? Gonna go play with your zis-and-zat baby friend?"

I got up and dusted myself off. I wanted to wallop Virgil real bad, but besides it going against Pappy's rules, I knew I had to skedaddle so I could go visit Mama.

"Scram," Paul told Virgil, standing with his tall self just about an inch from him. Paul could be downright menacing when he had a mind to be. Virgil's beady eyes were staring straight into Paul's chest. I was real grateful that Paul was there with me.

"We'll finish this later, lightnin' boy, when you don't have your dumber-than-dirt giant to protect you." Virgil kicked at the ground and walked away.

Soon as Virgil was outta sight, I thanked Paul and said see ya later. He went off toward his house, and I sprinted the rest of the way to Ridgely's, hoping Mama would be in good spirits today.

When we got to the jailhouse, Pappy and Mama greeted each other in their usual polite but stiffer-than-a-board way. Pappy left lickety-split, like he always did.

"You don't usually come visitin' so soon after y'all were just here, James. Anything wrong?" she asked.

I wasn't gonna tell her that the whole way to the jailhouse I'd had my fingers crossed that she'd be acting like her regular self. "No, Mama, nothin's wrong. I just wanted to see you. And, uh, I was wonderin' . . ."

"James, I need to talk to you about something first." Her eyes were bright, and she was looking straight at me, not down at the dirty floor like she did sometimes.

"You seem all right today, Mama. Are they letting you come home?"

"Not exactly, James. It's like this. So many days all I see is black and gray. Sometimes, life is so dark for me that I forget there are colors in the world. Today, I'm seein' all the colors of the rainbow. Even in this drab place, I'm seein' the pink in my fingernails, the yellow in my hair, and the green in your eyes. Do you get what I'm sayin', sweetie boy?"

"I don't guess I'm followin' you so good, Mama."

She was calm when she talked to me, just like the last time. She wasn't agitated like she sometimes got. And she wasn't brooding like other times.

"Sheriff Hammer says they can't keep me in this jail forever, but they can't let me go home neither. They're afraid I'll go on a binge and start losin' my head again. Bein' a menace to society is what the law calls it. I tried to convince him that I've learned my lesson. I told him I'd mind my p's and q's if he'd let me go home."

"So, you comin' home, Mama?" I crossed my fingers under the table.

"Not just yet, sweetie boy. Sheriff wouldn't budge. He's fixin' to send me to a place that's, uh . . . a place where he says I can get some help. For when I'm sinkin' into my dark times and . . . you know, when I have a hankerin' for the bottle."

"Where is this place, Mama?"

"It's kinda a distance from here. But I'm not gonna be there too long, so don't you worry none." She swiped the back of her hands across her eyes, which were welling up all of a sudden.

"What's this place called, Mama?"

"San Antonio State Hospital."

I started getting an ache in my belly bigger than all of Texas. I didn't understand how they could send Mama even farther away from me. All's I'd ever heard was that they sent people who weren't right in the head to that place. But I didn't dare tell Mama that.

"That's too far away," I said. "You don't need to go to no hospital. You sound fine to me." But then I remembered the visit before last, when she wouldn't say a word. She'd just stared at the concrete floor the whole time, wouldn't even look at me. Things musta been all black and gray for her that time.

"I'm not gonna be there forever, sweetie, I promise," she said. She laid her cold hand on mine. "I'm gonna come home to you all better. You'll see. I'm gonna be a new and improved version of your mama."

If this was gonna be a good thing for her, how come she kept tearing up?

"When you're better and all, are you gonna come live with me and Pappy?" I asked.

"I don't think so, sweetie. Your pappy and I are like oil and water. We don't mix too well. More'n likely, you and I will go back to livin' in our old house."

I was scared about her going away, but I'll admit I was also fretting about how it'd be when she came back. Would she start throwing those parties again with all the hollering and carrying on that got her in trouble in the first place? I wasn't gonna let on to Mama how much I was liking the quiet at Pappy's house, though.

Mama held my cheeks in her palms and eyeballed me. "Wasn't there something you wanted to ask me about?" she said.

I knew I went into that jailhouse bursting with questions, but it was like someone done took a blackboard eraser and wiped my head clean of all the things I'd wanted to ask Mama.

"How was she today?" Pappy asked after he fetched me from the jail.

"She was lookin' right at me, talkin' up a storm, actin' just fine," I said as I got in the truck. "But she says they're gonna send her to that hospital in San Antonio. Why can't we just bring her home?"

Pappy shook his head. "It's not that simple, Butch."

"But we can keep her away from the drink," I said.

The truck kicked up a mess of dust as we drove off from the jailhouse.

"It's more than just the drinkin' that troubles your mama. You know how sometimes when you go to see her, she hardly says a word? Just sits there, lookin' down, retreatin' inside herself. She gets in these moods as dark as a pocket. The doc says she's sufferin' from melancholia. They'll give her the help she needs at the hospital, so she can get better."

"How long's that gonna take, Pappy?"

"I don't rightly know the answer to that. We'll just have to be patient."

"Mama says that when she gets all better, me and her are gonna go back to livin' in our old house. Why can't she just come live with you and me? She says it won't work on account of you and her are oil and water."

"That's what she said, huh?" Pappy was quiet for a spell, staring at the road. "We'll see what we can work out after your mama gets well. Maybe she and I can move toward mixin' better, more like coffee and cream."

I shoved my hand inside my britches pocket and felt the charm from Abuela that I'd brought with me that afternoon. I had intended to ask Mama about it.

"I don't know why Mama wouldn't let Abuela treat her. I seen her cure people with my own eyes. In fact, Malvern was just tellin' me about how Abuela got him back on his feet when he was sick."

"She sure did, but he had nothin' more than a physical sickness. I'm afraid your mama's got mental suffering." He pointed to his head.

"That don't matter. Abuela told me that all illnesses are on account of the mind, the body, and the spirit being somehow outta balance. She said you can't heal one of those things without concern for the others. She even told me what Mama had wrong with her. Mama was sufferin' from *tristeza*."

"What's that mean, Butch?" Pappy asked.

"It meant she was still real sad about losing my daddy."

Pappy nodded. "I know your abuela tried to help her. Right after your daddy died, she offered your mama some special tea. And she wanted to do that ritual cleansing thing on her to get rid of your mama's negative energy and get her back into that balance you were talkin' about. But your mama wouldn't hear of it. She had it in her head that what your abuela did was all hokum."

By the time we pulled up to Ridgely's, the sun was sinking from view, spreading a thin line of orange across the sky. When we got outta the truck, I heard the screeching of a hawk and looked up to see it flying overhead. I hadn't seen a hawk since me and Paul were at the crater. I figured it must be a sign from the angels like Abuela once told me. And that's when I asked my last question that day. "Pappy, can we go visit Abuela's grave? I need to see her."

He looked away from me and stared down at his boots for what seemed like forever. Finally, he answered. "I suppose so. I'll take you over there tomorrow directly after school."

As far as I could figure, this was gonna be Pappy's first time going to see my abuela, his very own wife, since we'd buried her around six months before.

Chapter 12
A Stone for Abuela

The next day, the minute Miss Pritchert called, "Class dismissed!" and rang the bell, I raced outta the schoolhouse faster than a scalded cat. I didn't want to give Virgil even half a second to think about coming after me.

Soon as I got to Ridgely's, Pappy sent me over to our house to grab my jacket. I ran back to the diner with it and scooted into Pappy's truck, and we set out for Old Odessa Cemetery. It was a bumpy ride, and the whole way I could feel my lunch knocking around inside me.

"Sure wish they'd pave these roads," Pappy grumbled.

The cemetery was outside of town a ways. When we hopped outta the truck, Pappy looked up at the sky and knitted his brows together. "Those are some vicious clouds gatherin'. Don't like the look of 'em one bit. Put that jacket on, Butch, and let's make this snappy."

I knew what Pappy was thinking. Dark clouds could mean rain. And rain could mean lightning was coming. And lightning brought nothing but sorrow to my family. So rain clouds and Pappy were not on very good terms. And the thought of lightning got me shaking in my boots too. Even so, I didn't want to give up that visit.

We headed toward Abuela's grave. I had to run to keep up with Pappy's giant strides and so's I could hear what he was saying. He was telling me about how the oilmen sometimes drilled for oil—what everybody called "black gold"—in cemeteries.

"Why'd they do that, Pappy?" I asked. "Seems real disrespectful."

"Well, I reckon wildcatters are lookin' for oil in high places, thinkin' that gas pressure under the ground is what lifted those places up to begin with. And since most cemeteries are built on high ground, there's plenty of oil to be found in graveyards."

"Think they're gonna drill for oil here too?" I asked. "Right under Abuela's grave?"

"They just might try it, seein' as the dead can't rightly speak up to rebuke those drillers for disturbin' their rest. But don't you worry none. I don't mean to let that happen."

We weaved our way through the graveyard, passing by bouquets of flowers, all brown and dried up, sitting on top of a few of the graves. It was real quiet. Spooky quiet. I reckoned the dead couldn't make any noise. I slowed down to read some of the writing on the tombstones. A lotta them had religious stuff on them, like, "Asleep in Jesus" and "Gone to be with our Lord."

The gray clouds had filled up the whole sky and turned it a shade darker. Walking around where all those dead people were lying gave me the heebie-jeebies. It didn't help none when I noticed Pappy had gotten a ways ahead of me.

"Over here!" he called.

I ran to catch up to him and found him standing over Abuela's grave. Instead of a cross like all the others in the graveyard, her headstone had two hands in a praying position carved on it. The writing said, *Marlena Olivera Ridgely, born 1874, died 1927. Tender wife, mother, grandmother, and healer.* And right next to her was my daddy. His headstone had the dates and said, *James Joshua Ridgely. Loving husband, father, and son. Taken too young.*

Pappy picked up two small stones from the ground and, as gently as if they were made of glass, set one on top of each grave. There was already a whole collection of little rocks on top of my daddy's grave. I glanced around the graveyard and didn't see rocks on any of the other graves.

"Whatya do that for, Pappy?" I asked.

"Whenever we came here to visit your daddy, your abuela set a stone on his grave. Before she passed, she asked me to put a stone on her grave and on JJ's, to signify I was here. I'm honorin' her wishes."

I picked up a coupla stones and put one on my daddy's grave and one on Abuela's. Pappy nodded his approval.

"You know, don't you, that there's nothin' on this earth I wouldn't do for your abuela? I owe her my life."

"How do ya mean?" I'd heard plenty of stories about Abuela saving people in town, but I didn't know nothing about her saving Pappy's life.

Pappy looped his long arm around my shoulders as we stood over Abuela's grave. It surprised me since Pappy wasn't the affectionate sort, as Mama would say. With Pappy's strong arm protecting me, I felt a little less spooked being near all those dead folks.

"Well, Butch, it goes back to how your abuela and I first met."

"Did y'all meet at the diner?" I asked.

"No, this was quite a while before I ever opened the diner. When I first came out from Virginia to Odessa as a young man, I got me a job layin' tracks for the Texas and Pacific Railway Company."

It was hard for me to picture the railroad as not always being there.

"How did you meet Abuela then?" I asked.

"One day, I was toilin' away on the tracks, and I took sick. I was so darn weak that I just keeled over. The other guys on the tracks told me later that they thought I was a goner. Somebody went and fetched this young lady who was known for her healing powers. The guys carried me to a nearby shack and laid me out." Pappy looked up and studied the clouds.

"Did she pat eggs and lemons on your body?" I asked. "I seen her do that with some of the folks she was healin' when she let me tag along."

"I was barely conscious, so I've only got a hazy memory of what she did for me. I do remember her spreadin' my arms out so my body looked like a cross. The guys who took me to her told me later that she ran an egg over me, then cracked the egg in a glass of water and examined what was inside that glass. It seems that's how she figured what I was sufferin' from."

"I remember her doin' that same thing on me when I was real little. After Daddy died," I said. "How'd she know what was ailin' someone from an egg floatin' around in water? That's somethin' she never explained to me."

"Don't rightly know. My guess is you've got far more knowledge on the subject than I ever could. I think you might have the healin' powers runnin' through you too."

"How do ya figure, Pappy?"

"Well, for a little guy, you sure seem to have a sense of when someone's feelin' poorly, and I've heard you suggestin' to folks what it is that might be ailin' them. I know your abuela sent you out sometimes to pick her special herbs, and she said you always came back with just what she needed."

"Do ya think Abuela was trainin' me to be a healer?"

"No doubt she recognized that you more'n likely inherited her special talent." Pappy stared up at the

dark gray sky with a wrinkled brow like he was trying to will it to hold back the rain.

"Did she do anythin' else for you when you were
laid up?"

"Last thing they told me she did was sweep a
bundle of herbs over my body. And she stayed with
me every night, callin' on the spirits for healing. She
threw thick blankets over me to make me sweat and
said some prayers."

I felt a few drops of rain. Pappy took his arm off
my shoulders and sharply turned me in the direction
of where we had parked.

"God's spittin' on us," he said, shaking his finger
at the sky. "This is gonna be a real toad-strangler.
Let's get outta here before the deluge."

Most of the time, it was so dry in Odessa even
the catfish were carrying canteens, as Pappy liked to
say. So, when a storm saw fit to come, it was gonna
be a doozy.

Pappy grabbed my hand, and we high-tailed it
back through the graveyard toward the truck. Suddenly, the sky opened up and Pappy and I were
soaked to the bone by the time we got there. My
socks were squishy wet, and cold drops were dripping off the tip of my nose. At least we got ourselves

inside the truck where we could keep from getting any wetter.

"Thank the Lord I traded in that old Ford TT and got us a truck with a closed cab," Pappy said after he pulled the driver's-side door closed. "That old thing was completely open to the heavens."

Ever since my daddy had gotten struck down by lightning, Mama and now Pappy made sure to get me far from any place that lightning might hit whenever a storm was brewing. Pappy taught me that the worst place to be was anywhere up high, and that it was safest to be inside a house or a car.

The rain pounding on the truck's metal roof sounded like bullets pelting it. Even so, I felt safe inside the truck. But I was getting the shivers from being so wet. I hugged my body, trying to warm up a little. Pappy musta seen me shaking.

"Soon as we get to the diner, we'll grab some towels and get you dried off good," he said. "But we gotta stop there 'fore we go home, so we can sandbag the door, or we'll be servin' nothin' but rainwater to the customers."

"Sure, Pappy."

Since Pappy was in a rare talking mood and I needed something to think about besides how cold and wet I was, I started up my questioning again. And besides, I needed to hear the rest of the story about him meeting Abuela for the first time.

"What happened when Abuela finished performin' her healin' on you?" I asked. "Were you all better after that?"

"It took about a week 'fore I was sittin' up. The fever finally left me. And as soon as I had my wits about me, which took a few more days, I asked your abuela to marry me. I guess you could say me gettin' sick was the best thing ever happened to me. That's how the Lord brought me your grandmother." Pappy took one hand off the wheel to wipe the rain off his cheeks. Or was it tears he was wiping? I couldn't tell.

Driving back, our tires were sloshing through mud on account of the dips in the road were filling up with water. I was getting tossed around in my seat. The rain was coming down so hard and fast that the windshield wipers couldn't keep up with it, and that made it hard for Pappy to see through the window. It was one of those angry storms where the rain went on a rampage, gushing down the roads and sweeping up everything unlucky enough to be in its way. From the truck, I caught sight of a fence post, some shrubs, and a meowing cat being carried down the street by the rushing water.

Suddenly, there was a flash in the sky. I looked over at Pappy. His face was whiter than chalk, and his hands were gripping the steering wheel like if he didn't hold tight, it was gonna get washed away with everything else. He counted the seconds out loud till the thunder roared. That's how we could tell how far away the lightning was. My belly started hurting.

Pappy finally pulled up at Ridgely's and turned off the engine. But we stayed put in the truck. We waited, on the lookout for more lightning. There was another flash. Pappy yelled, "Let's get inside quick!"

The water was already seeping in under the doorway of the diner. Soon as we got inside and pulled the door shut, Pappy whistled out a huge sigh. I took a real deep breath.

"You picked a heck of a time to go visiting your abuela, James. Now run and fetch the sandbags!" Pappy shouted while he grabbed a mop from the kitchen.

I ran to the storage closet to get the sandbags. The floor was wet and slippery, so my feet slid out from under me and I went flying. I landed real hard on my behind and let out a yelp. Pappy came running and found me on the floor.

"You okay, Butch?" he asked, helping me up. "You're gonna find yourself with some bruises on your rear end as colorful as a Texas sunset." I was pretty certain he was smiling under that beard of his. And some color was coming back to his face.

I limped over to help him stack up the sandbags outside the diner door. Then he threw me some kitchen towels, and I dried myself off as best I could. After he finished mopping up the floor, we put the CLOSED sign out. Not that we needed to. I didn't suspect anyone else in town woulda been foolish enough to be out in that gusher.

Chapter 13
Eatin' and Jawin' at Paul's House

The very next day, it was back to being drier outside than a popcorn fart. That's probably why people were always saying, "If you don't like the weather in Texas, wait a minute." Since most of the streets in Odessa were nothing but dirt, not paved at all, and fulla ditches, the storm left puddles as deep as swimming holes. To keep my feet dry walking to and from school, I pulled on my mama's old boots. She used to wear them so's she could hide her flask of moonshine inside, them being real loose on top. I knew because I caught her slipping in a flask more than once. 'Course, she didn't get to bring the boots to jail with her. Considering how big they looked on my feet, it didn't surprise me none when Virgil went and opened his big trap about them.

"You steal them boots off a dead giant?" he said.

I didn't give two hoots about Virgil's opinion. I woulda rather worn my mama's shoes and had dry feet all day than be wearing Virgil's shoes, which anybody coulda seen were downright soggy. Besides, wearing Mama's boots was the best way I knew for me to feel like she was still being a mama to me. At least she was keeping my feet dry.

In the afternoon, Pappy let me quit work early 'cause I was invited over to Paul's for supper. Paul told me his family was having a special meal to celebrate some holiday or another and that his mama wanted me to come on account of she thought I'd especially like the food that she and Bubby were cooking up. But I thought maybe the real reason she wanted me to come was so's she could get to know Paul's friends. And seeing as I was his only friend, that meant me.

Standing outside Paul's house, I heard hollering before I even knocked. But not angry hollering, mind you. It was louder in that house than Pappy's Sunday tie. Even though I'd been there before, I hesitated at the front door on account of the last time there was so much commotion and I didn't understand what they were going on about most of the time since they spoke a different language.

I finally got up my nerve to knock. Paul opened the door, wearing a black hat with a brim that I'd never seen him wear before. His little sister, Frieda, came running over to greet me too. She was okay for a girl. I reckoned her big, round, dark eyes had seen a lot in her six years, considering her coming all the way over to the United States, a whole different country, and having to learn a new language and all. Truth was, her English was better than Paul's. You couldn't hardly tell she wasn't from these parts. She was about the age I was when my daddy got struck by lightning.

I took a step into the house, and Frieda smiled at me. She was missing one of her front teeth. "*Gut yontiff*, James," she said.

"Huh?"

"I am wishing you a 'good holiday' because tonight is our New Year's," Frieda said. She had on a plaid dress that looked nicer than what she usually wore. Her raven-black hair was tucked into a kerchief like usual, but her frizzy curls didn't like to stay put, and they were poking out all over the place.

"Whatya mean by New Year's?" I asked. "It's only October. Unless somethin' changed, the new year don't start until January 1."

"We have our own New Year's holiday that's starting now. It's when we celebrate the birthday of the whole world," Frieda explained.

Paul's mama yelled something from the kitchen.

"Muter says to tell you dinner is almost ready," Frieda said.

"Something smells mighty fine," I said. "What's your mama cookin'?"

"I don't know how you call this food in English, but I think you'll like it. I helped Muter and Bubby make it."

Paul's stepfather, Samuel, and his uncle Ruvin were standing over by the dining table, wagging their fingers at each other and speaking their language with raised voices. That night, instead of their bowler hats, they wore what looked like furry critters on their heads. I musta looked at them funny 'cause Paul said, "We wear these hats special for holiday."

"Hello, James," Paul's mama said, coming outta their tiny kitchen, wiping her hands on the stained-up green apron tied around her waist. "You see I try for learning English. Pinkus and Frieda, they explain me many words."

It was the first time she had ever said anything to me in English. Even though she never smiled with her mouth, I coulda sworn she was smiling at me with her eyes. That made her okay in my book. *You'll know someone's heart if you peer into their eyes*, Mama always said.

Paul's mama had rings around her eyes like the rings that rippled in the pond when I skipped rocks in it. Everything about her was dark, excepting her cotton-white skin. Her hair was the color of the coffee Pappy poured at the diner. Her eyes were just as black, and she wore the plainest, darkest clothes I ever did see. And when she was speaking in her language, even her words came out in a dark, serious-sounding way.

You couldn't have found two people more different than Paul's mama and my mama. Except when she was having one of her bad spells, Mama was hardly ever serious. She laughed like a pack of hyenas, and people called her "mighty colorful." I knew they weren't referring to her red lipstick or her green eyes neither. I a-feared if I ever introduced our mamas to each other, Paul's mama might be so shocked by how colorful my mama was that she'd head straight for the hills.

While we stood in the living room, waiting on supper to be ready, I looked around. In the corner there was a big, low wooden table where Paul's uncle and stepfather, who were both tailors, did their sewing and mending. Swatches of cloth, pairs of scissors, and boxes of buttons and needles were piled up on the table, and the shelf underneath was covered with bolts of material. When I'd been at Paul's house before, I'd seen Samuel sitting cross-legged on top of that table, hunched over a pair of trousers or something else he was pulling a needle through.

Against the wall, there was a tall bookcase with ancient-looking books crowding its bookshelves, a pair of tarnished silver candlesticks, and a whole row of egg-shaped ceramic dolls going from teeny-tiny to bigger and bigger and bigger, as if each one could fit inside the next bigger-sized one. I also noticed—squeezed in between some of the books—an old, worn-looking brass candleholder with spaces for a bunch of candles. It looked like something I'd seen before somewhere.

I was fixing to ask Paul about it, but just then Paul's bubby came outta the kitchen and pushed us over to the dining table. Me and all of Paul's family stood by the table while Frieda brought around a plate of sliced apples and a small bowl of something.

"Take a piece of apple and dip it in this honey," Frieda told me, offering me the bowl. "It's for a sweet new year."

While everybody was holding an apple slice dripping with honey, Uncle Ruvin said some words in another language. Then Paul whispered to me, "You can eat it now."

After they licked their sticky fingers, they kissed each other's cheeks and said, "Gut yontiff" to one another. Then Bubby came up behind me and pressed down hard on my shoulders till I understood that she wanted me to sit. The mouthwatering smells went a long way toward making me forget my sore behind, which was still smarting from my fall at Ridgely's the day before.

"*Ess, ess, mayn kind!*" Paul's mama said to me as she set the food on the table. She served us these little square, doughy things that looked like stuffed cookies. I took a bite, thinking it was gonna be sweet, but instead my mouth got a real surprise when I discovered it had meat inside. Paul's aunt Yetta put out steaming bowls of chicken soup with triangle-shaped noodle pouches floating in the broth. I'd never seen anything like it before, and it sure was tasty. Paul's mama and aunt Yetta finally sat at the table after putting out a dish that tasted like a mixture of pickles and cabbage. It was too dang sour for me and left me with a downright bumpy tongue. The only food I recognized were the taters, seeing as Pappy was always cooking up potatoes in all different ways at the diner.

The grown-ups kept passing bowls of food to me. No one was ever gonna starve in that house.

"*Ess, ess,*" they said, even while they were asking me questions in their not-so-perfect English. And I kept ess, ess-ing and trying to answer their questions between bites. It was hard 'cause I was trying to mind my manners and not talk with my mouth full, like my mama had taught me.

Uncle Ruvin was sitting next to me. He looked at me with deep brown eyes that I was sure my mama woulda said were *kind eyes.* "What does your fazer do?" he asked.

Paul said something to him in their language, and Uncle Ruvin patted my arm and said, "Oh, I am very sorry. And muter?"

Again, Paul said something to him.

"*Oy veh!*" Paul's mama cried and clapped her cheeks. The others shook their heads and looked down at their plates.

"Oh," Ruvin said.

"It's okay. Mama's goin' to a hospital to get better," I said. "And when she does, she'll come home. Meanwhile, my pappy and I manage just fine. He owns Ridgely's Diner, but I guess you knew that already." Paul translated what I said.

"What did your mama do to get put in jail?" Frieda asked. Paul shook his head and narrowed his eyes at her.

"It's okay, Paul," I said. "There's no keepin' secrets in this town. Mama got too attached to the giggle water she was gettin' from the bootleggers. She got a little carried away is how my pappy explains it." Paul didn't bother translating that time.

"Wow," Frieda said. Frieda's English was so good that she could even pronounce her w's.

"But it wasn't real fair that they locked up my mama for her drinkin', considerin' what I heard tell about Senator Morris Sheppard," I said, by way of defending Mama.

"What is it you hear about the senator?" Uncle Ruvin asked. Since he and his wife, Yetta, had come to the States a few years before Paul's mama and Samuel, Ruvin's English was better than theirs. In fact, Ruvin's English was downright good.

"He's the one who wrote the law against drinkin'

in the first place," I explained. "Real quick after they passed Prohibition in Texas—the law the senator himself wrote—folks found out he had a still on his farm that was puttin' out a whole lotta whiskey every day!"

"He sounds like he wants to make it against law for everybody but himself to sell alcohol, so he make all the money." Ruvin shook his head. "Is same corruption we left behind in our country. The government people there make the laws to help themselves. And they do not follow their own laws."

I don't think the other grown-ups understood the conversation at all, so the women took up saying "Ess, ess!" again and passing me plates of food.

I ate so much I was liable to burst. I just couldn't *ess* anymore.

"Let's go for walk," Paul said, saving me from popping like an overblown balloon.

Before we left, I took another gander at that candleholder on the bookshelf. My mind got stuck on where I mighta seen it before. Soon as Paul and I got outside, I asked, "Hey Paul, that brass candlestick that you've got on the shelf with the books—it looks pretty old. What is it exactly?"

"Is something for candles that Muter brought from our country. You are right—it is very old. It belong to the bubby of my bubby."

"I can't rightly place it, but it looks awful familiar. Mind if I ask your mama about it?"

"Next time you come," Paul said. We talked while he walked me partway back to my house. It was pretty dark outside, but the moon was a ball of light helping us make out the path.

"Pappy's finally gonna let me go do somethin' fun after church on Sunday," I told him. "I'm through bein' grounded. Wanna hike to the crater with me?"

"I would, yes."

"I know you told me that we don't have your kinda church here, but does that mean you don't have to go to any church at all, ever? Not even for Sunday school?" I asked.

"We do not go to church. They have what is our kinda church in Galveston, the first place we came to in Texas. But is too far away for us. Anyway, my stepfather always says *love in the home is more important than prayer in the temple.* So is okay that we don't go."

"Lucky duck," I said. "Did you have to go to church when you were growin' up in that Odessa where you came from?"

Paul shook his head and didn't say anything. Then he started shifting from one leg to the other, and I saw his *No Trespassing* sign go up, so I didn't ask him any more about church.

"I'll come fetch you after church on Sunday, after I grab us some eats from my house," I told him. "And this time, we gotta head back way before sundown, so's we don't get in trouble again. And so's you don't get hit in the tuchas with a teakettle."

Paul smiled his half smile and turned to walk back home.

Chapter 14
Makin' a Pact

Reverend Crawford rarely had anything interesting to say, if you ask me. The only thing that motivated me to walk into First Christian Church, besides the fact that Pappy made me, was the chance to catch a glimpse of Fanny Crawford. 'Course she had no choice but to be there on account of her father being the reverend and all.

And I usually made an effort to listen to his sermons so I could have something to talk to Fanny about. I wasn't too good with talking to girls. Pappy said girls weren't always easy to understand but that when I got older I might be able to figure them out.

I perked up when I heard the reverend preaching: "Some folks have more money and some folks have less, but faith—faith is free. There's no charge for faith, my friends. If you believe and follow the ways of our Lord, you will be rich."

That's when I tapped Pappy and whispered, "If faith is free, how come they're always passin' around the collection basket in church?"

"Shush, James," Pappy said, elbowing me in the ribs.

Soon as the closing hymn was sung, I raced outta church and ran home to pick up the food I'd packed for our hike. Then I fetched Paul.

"How was church?" Paul asked me soon as we headed off for the crater. I guess he was curious on account of it wasn't a place he ever had to go.

"Church is church. It don't hold my interest none. I come out here, where it's quiet, nobody yappin' at me, and I do my own prayin'. Inside my head. Reverend Crawford wants us to have faith in Jesus, but when the important people in your life get taken away, it's kinda hard to have faith in anything. Know what I mean?"

"Yes, I understand. What they say in church when your father was killed?" Paul asked.

"The reverend told me and my mama that my daddy was gone to be with Jesus in heaven. That's pretty much what he says whenever anybody goes and dies."

"What happens in heaven?" Those dark eyes of Paul's were holding on to my face real tight.

"I was so little when my daddy died, I don't rightly remember what the reverend said when I asked him what's it like up in heaven. But the other place—the place down below—that's one subject Reverend Crawford goes on about a lot. He says sinners end up writhin' in all these flames. But what I wanna know is how does he know that? Was he there himself? 'Course I can't ask him that. I'd get my hide tanned for disrespecting the reverend. And besides, I'd kinda like to get on his good side."

"I know why you say this. I see you in classroom—you stare at Fanny Crawford." Paul gave me a friendly punch on the shoulder.

I shrugged. "She's all right, I guess."

We hiked in silence for a while, trying not to stumble over the rocks or fall into any buffalo wallows this time. Aside from a meadowlark warbling some, it was as quiet as a graveyard out there. We didn't pass much else that was alive, excepting a lizard here and there playing hide-and-seek in the rocks and a coupla horned toads.

"What is wrong with those trees?" Paul broke our silence, pointing at some mesquite trees. "Something not right how the branches are falling."

"They've been attacked by twig girdlers."

"What means twig girdler?"

"They're these beetles that get inside the trees, makin' the leaves turn all brown and die. Then the branches bend down like old men and break off. It's a real shame what they do to the trees. Guess you didn't have any of those in your Odessa."

"No, I never saw this kinda beetles," Paul said, staring off into space without blinking.

I snapped my fingers in front of his eyes. "Where'd you go, Paul?"

He shook his head back and forth. "I was just thinking that here in America people worry about something that attacks your trees. In Ukraine, we not have time to worry about trees. We worry about something that attacks people."

"Those must be some giant beetles if they're goin' after people," I said.

"Not beetles." Paul started walking faster. I had to take two steps for each one of his just to keep up. "We get attacked by the army in my country."

"Why would your army attack their own people?"

"I do not know," Paul answered in almost a whisper. He balled up his hands into tight fists and picked up his pace even more.

"Hey, slow down, wouldya!" I called. "You wanna set for a spell and eat?" Something had gotten Paul all riled up, and I figured it was a good time to change the subject. Besides, my stomach was starting to do some right loud rumbling.

"Okay," he said. He stopped walking and unclenched his fists. "I can eat."

I had packed plenty for both of us: ham sandwiches, salted peanuts, apples, and Pappy's home-baked sugar cookies. We plopped ourselves on the ground under a mesquite tree, it being the only shade anywhere around. I handed Paul a sandwich. He lifted a corner of the bread and took a peek inside.

"No thanks," he said and passed the sandwich back to me.

"Come on, take it," I said. "I thought you were hungry. Pappy made 'em for us."

"I not eat ham," he said.

"That's funny—my abuela didn't like ham either."

Paul had no trouble eating the other food I brought, though. Paul had what Pappy called "one hearty appetite." Maybe it was 'cause he had such a tall body to feed.

While we were filling up our bellies, and seeing as Paul had calmed down, I decided to try another question. "What you said before about that army didn't make any sense to me. Isn't an army supposed to protect the people in a country from their enemies?"

"I think so, but is not what this army did. Mostly soldiers—called Cossacks—they hate Jews and blame them for everything bad in my country." Paul's voice rose in anger. "They love to yell, 'Strike at the Zhyds and save Russia!' Zhyds is what they call Jews." He stared at the ground.

I started working on my second ham sandwich, the one meant for Paul. "Did the Jews do somethin' bad?" I asked.

Paul jumped up like his britches were on fire and hollered at me, "No! They do nothing wrong! These Cossacks are cruel and make trouble for no reason. You not understand!" He pounded the air with his fist as if he was punching his worst enemy right in the kisser.

"What're you so sore about? Do you know some Jews who these soldiers attacked?"

Paul sat back down. His face looked even paler than usual. He stared at the ground and wouldn't look me in the eye. "Us. They attack all of us."

"You mean your family before you came here?" There was a colony of ants marching in a ruler-straight line on the ground between us. Paul kept his eyes fixed on the parade.

"Yes, I am talking about my family. They attack us because we are Jews."

Hearing Paul say that he was a Jew took me by surprise. I guess I hadn't thought much about what religion Paul mighta been. This probably explained why his family didn't go to any of the churches we had in town—and why Paul's family had some different kinda holidays than we did, like their own New Year's. I'd figured it was a holiday they celebrated in their country. But I really knew next to nothing about Jews, excepting that if you believed what some people said, they killed Christ. And I heard the oilmen grumbling sometimes about the Jews being moneygrubbing. But that sure didn't describe Paul's family none. Anyhow, Mama was always telling me not to believe everything I heard.

The ants were carrying crumbs from our sugar cookies while they marched.

"It not bother you to know that I am Jewish?" Paul asked.

"Why would I give two hoots that you're Jewish? Heck, you still wanted to be my friend even though most everybody else thinks I'm cursed."

Some pink found its way back to Paul's cheeks. He looked up at me instead of fixing his eyes on the marching ants and even gave me a quick half smile. We had polished off the food, so I said, "Let's get goin'. We still got a load of walkin' to do."

When we got to the crater, we stood on the edge. We were looking down into the giant hole when I got the idea that we could say whatever we wanted to and just leave our words in that hole where nobody else could hear them.

"How 'bout we make a pact that nothin' we say here at the crater gets talked about anywhere else?" I said. "Nobody gets to know what we say here."

"I agree. Is good idea."

"Shake on it?" I grabbed Paul's big hand. "First we gotta spit in our shakin' hands."

We put out our spit-on hands to shake. While I shook his hand, I tapped the inside of his palm three times with my middle finger. "From now on, that's gonna be our secret handshake. We can never break a deal that's sealed with this handshake."

With our hands still clasped, Paul tapped my palm three times with his middle finger. "Like this?" he asked.

"Yup," I said. "Now it's like we got our very own club. And this here crater's our clubhouse." We dropped our hands and stood next to each other on the edge of the crater, staring down into it.

"First time my pappy took me here, he read me a poem called *The Rime of the Ancient Mariner*," I told Paul. "This poet fella wrote it about a meteor shower he saw before you and me were even alive. Pappy and I'd read that poem together the coupla times we came out to the crater."

Anybody else woulda made awful fun of me for even talking about poetry. They woulda teased me for being too girly. But I knew as sure as it wasn't gonna snow in the summer that Paul wouldn't laugh at me. So I wasn't surprised none when he said, "I would like to hear that poem sometime."

A hawk started screeching and we both looked up to see it circling. I wondered if the bird was Abuela's spirit bringing me a message, but I couldn't figure what that message would be.

"Do ya think these bits of the solar system, like

the ones that crashed down to make this big ole hole, are fallin' to earth for a reason? Sometimes I think maybe that's where heaven is—out there with the stars and planets," I said and picked up a rock and threw it as far as I could into the crater. "Maybe the Lord is tossin' these pieces down to remind us that we're just little dots on this giant planet and that there's somethin' loads more powerful than us out there."

"Maybe God look down at us same way we look down at tiny ants," Paul said. "We can step on them or we can leave them alone."

"I wonder why God sometimes decides to step on us instead of leavin' us be."

"What are you meaning?" Paul asked.

"For starters, why would God let my daddy get struck by lightnin'? If he decides to let lightnin' strike, ain't nothin' any of us can do about it. My daddy didn't do anythin' bad."

"We can run from the lightning, yes?" Paul said.

"My daddy couldn't. But yeah, I guess there's some bad stuff we can run from. Seems like your family could run away to be safe. And Pappy wants me to skedaddle from Virgil when he's after me. But maybe it'd be better if we threw some lightnin' bolts of our own first, instead of always havin' to run from the lightnin'.''

"You mean to fight back?"

"Yeah. Why not? Just because I'm not allowed to use my fists don't mean you can't. You're way bigger than Virgil, and you could clobber him next time he tries somethin'." I shot a fist in the air.

"But my *muter* and Samuel say I must not make trouble. Anyway, Virgil Jackson is nothing but a *shmendrick*. Is somebody that is not worth thinking about and even less worth fighting."

"Maybe that's true about Virgil," I said. "But what if you need to defend yourself? Do you even know how to fight?"

"Yes. When we first arrive to Texas Odessa, Uncle Ruvin teach me how to box. He tells me maybe I will have problems in school and I need protect myself."

I couldn't picture thin, pale, white-bearded Uncle Ruvin knowing the first thing about boxing. If I'd seen him on the street, I woulda thought he was some kinda professor.

"I get it," I said. "Even though Pappy won't let me fight, I reckon he'd have no objection to me learnin' how to protect myself. Can you teach me some moves? Strictly for defendin' myself, mind you."

So right then and there above the crater, Paul gave me boxing lessons. He showed me how to move back and forth, like I was doing a dance, and how to duck my head and protect my face. I was no Jack Dempsey, but I picked it up pretty quick. We danced around, punching and blocking in the air, careful not to get too close to the edge of the crater.

Remembering the trouble we got in the last time, we kept an eye on the sun and left before it started setting so as to give ourselves plenty of daylight for the hike home.

Chapter 15
Teachin' Virgil Jackson a Lesson

Virgil tormenting Paul and me—before school, in school, and after school—got to be as regular a part of our day as learning the three R's. Calling us names like "Bootleg Baby" and "The Dumb Giant," he thought he was so clever he near broke his arm patting himself on the back.

With Paul being so much bigger than Virgil, Virgil wouldn't dare pick a fistfight with him, especially if Virgil didn't have his posse around. That sure saved me some beatings. But whenever Paul wasn't in sight, Virgil went after me like I was a rented mule. At least after my boxing lessons, I knew how to block a punch. But that didn't keep me from getting knocked down when Virgil shoved me.

One day, after Virgil had sent me tumbling to

the ground, Paul found me and helped me up. "It is enough, James," he said. "We must make him stop."

Paul's words were mighty welcome. I'd decided I'd had my fill of Virgil and that it was time to teach him a lesson. I told Paul the plan I'd cooked up. Then we spit on our hands and did our secret handshake.

On Sunday after church, Paul and I went off in search of twig girdlers. I knew we'd find plenty over by the Henchleys' pecan groves, seeing as how those long-horned beetles love digging into pecan trees the best. Using sticks, we scraped as many of the beetles as we could into a gunnysack.

Next day, I brought the sack with me to school and hid it behind a mesquite tree outside of the schoolhouse. Paul and I waited till lunch recess. Everybody ran outside to play kickball or red rover. In the yard, Virgil came up to me, grabbed my arm and twisted it around behind me.

"Let's see you get outta this, lightnin' boy," he said.

Margaret, Elmer, and Earl gathered around him like he was the king of Odessa. I never could cotton on to why they even followed Virgil. He had a mean streak running from the top of his head to the tip of his big toe. While Virgil held my arm in a twist, Paul went to get the sack we'd hidden.

"Let go of James," Paul ordered him, with the sack in his hand.

Virgil looked up at Paul. He musta been feeling real brave with his posse there, 'cause he snarled, "You gonna make me, Mister Zis and Zat?"

Paul came up behind him and stretched out the back of Virgil's overalls. He shook those twig girdlers from the sack right inside Virgil's britches where the sun don't shine.

"What in tarnation—!" Virgil yelped and let go of my arm lickety-split. The other kids jumped back like they were scared the girdlers were gonna leap into their britches next. It was a sight all right. Virgil started hopping and squealing like a pig fulla Mexican jumping beans.

"Hey Virgil," I said, "we just thought you oughtta get to know these twig girdlers, seein' as you've got things in common—you're both big pests and 'bout as pleasant as an outhouse breeze."

"You'll pay for this, lightnin' boy!" he hollered, shaking himself and swatting at his back. Then he yelled at Paul, "I'll get you too, you dumb Christ killer."

His posse stood around at a safe distance, pointing and snickering and not offering to help him none. While I knew our troubles with Virgil weren't near over, I was enjoying watching him squirm. Paul threw me one of his crooked grins. And best of all, Fanny came over to see what all the commotion was about. She could hardly swallow her giggling. She smiled at me, and all's I wanted to do was touch that dimple on her cheek to see how deep it went. 'Course I woulda never done that.

By the time the bell rang at the end of recess, Virgil had run off—or more like hopped away, wriggling as he went. He didn't come back to school that day.

When I got to Ridgely's after school, I was bursting to tell someone about what we did to Virgil. But I knew Pappy wouldn't approve. In his book, what me and Paul did woulda fallen into the category of "makin' trouble."

I was real glad when Malvern came in for dinner and he sat at a table instead of up at the counter where Pappy woulda heard every word we said. I plopped myself down at his table. Keeping my voice real low, I said, "Got somethin' to tell you, but you gotta promise not to tell Pappy." I shared the story of Virgil and the twig girdlers with Malvern. I knew if anybody would appreciate what we did, it'd be Malvern.

"I guess you showed him that you can dish it out too, huh?" Malvern said. He was shoveling in forkfuls of his favorite meal on the menu—stewed chicken with biscuit dumplings. "Speakin' of dishin' it out, why don't we have some apple pie in honor of your little prank today, Butch?"

When he called me Butch, it made me feel all grown up, since most of the oil guys had nicknames too—like Soldier Boy, Lemonhead, and Bugbee. Malvern was just plain Malvern, though.

"That'd be mighty fine," I said. "Ain't nothin' better than Pappy's apple pie."

I snuck a look at Malvern's hand with its missing fingers wrapped around his coffee cup, and I thought about how badly I wanted to keep all ten of my own.

Malvern musta caught me looking at his hand. "Now I've got a story for you, Butch. I ever tell you about how I lost my fingers?"

"Nope, I don't believe so." I'd been wanting to ask for a long time, but I figured Malvern wouldn't be too keen on digging up that painful memory.

"It happened back when I was workin' as a doodlebug, locatin' the oil. We were drivin' the nitroglycerin—the explosives—over to the spot where I knew the oil was hidin'. But we never made it. Soon as we hit a bump in the road, the explosives went off. I was blown clear across the field." Malvern held up his three-fingered hand. "But I was lucky enough to walk away with only a couple less fingers."

I musta turned ghost white 'cause Malvern patted my hand and said, "Maybe I shouldn'ta told you that story. Didn't mean to shock you none. You oughtta know, though, that some jobs in this black gold business can be downright dangerous."

Just then Pappy came over to the table.

"James, I didn't see you come in," he said. "Could use some help back in the kitchen."

"Okay if I buy this boy a slice of apple pie, Jeb, before he gets to work?" Malvern asked.

"I suppose so. You want a piece for yourself, Malvern?"

"You betcha," Malvern said.

After Pappy went to get the pie, I said, "If I end up being a wildcatter, I'm gonna lead the drillers to the oil, but then I'm gonna skedaddle long before they go callin' for the explosives. Ya think I could be an oilman, Malvern?"

"I reckon you could, Butch, but from where I sit, it seems to me you could do a whole lot more with all those brains of yours."

Pappy set down two slices of pie and told me to come to the kitchen as soon as I finished eating. I took a forkful. The pie was still warm, and the gooey apple filling made my mouth tingle.

With a mouth fulla pie, I asked Malvern, "If I'm not gonna be an oilman, what should I be, do ya think? Don't tell Pappy, but I'm not keen on spendin' the rest of my life workin' in the diner."

"Looky here, I don't know if the thought ever occurred to you, but I wonder if you might like to be a healer like your abuela. Or a doctor. I've noticed you takin' a keen interest in your abuela's remedies," he said, wiping away some pie crumbs from the corners of his mouth. "At any rate, you've got to follow your own path, boy."

"How am I gonna know what my path is?" I scraped up every last bit of apple stuck to my plate.

"Well, sometimes you're best off lookin' behind you first, seein' where you've come from, before you decide where you're headed."

I didn't exactly get what Malvern was driving at. Sometimes trying to understand grown-ups was tougher than solving a Hardy Boys mystery. But Malvern's words did get me to wondering. What if some of the stuff that happened in my past, like my daddy's death and watching Abuela perform her healing and my mama being taken away, all got stirred up together to lead me to finding my purpose?

I decided then and there that I'd try again to get Pappy to explain some things to me. And maybe I'd even get some help from Mama too, when she was having one of her good days.

Chapter 16
Nature Teachin' Us a Lesson

"Phew! In this heat, the hens are sure to be layin' hard-boiled eggs," Pappy said at church the next Sunday as he wiped sweat off his brow.

Considering fall had almost come and gone, it wasn't supposed to be so warm still. The ladies were wearing their veils to protect their faces from the boiling hot winds. It wasn't much cooler inside the church neither. And worst of all, I didn't catch sight of Fanny in the pews. She musta been feeling poorly if she was skipping church.

I was even less in the mood for Reverend Crawford's preaching than usual. This time he was going on about forgiveness.

Before my mind wandered off, I heard the beginning of the reverend's sermon. "Did Judas the Jew, who was hired by the Jewish priests to betray his friend Jesus for thirty pieces of silver, merit forgiveness? After all, this betrayal led to Jesus's death on the cross. But Christ's forgiveness is not dependent on our behavior," he said.

I think the real reason the reverend was addressing the whole forgiveness subject was 'cause a lotta the white-haired folks had just gotten swindled outta their money by a traveling salesman. He'd been selling some kinda potion that was supposed to make all your aches and pains disappear. Pappy said he was nothing but a fakeloo artist and that some of the ladies woulda bought Texas dirt from him, on account of they all thought he was the most handsome man who ever set foot in Odessa. He'd charmed them into buying up his potion with his grin as wide as Texas. Problem was, soon as they drank it they got sicker than dogs.

Maybe instead of preaching about forgiveness, the reverend shoulda been warning those folks not to trust a man who's got a permanent grin on his face. If Abuela had still been alive, she woulda set them straight. And if they'd got themselves fooled by that phonus-bolonus smile and gone and bought the tonic anyways, Abuela coulda healed them right up after they got sick from it.

I'm sure she woulda. After my daddy died, I was in a sorry state. I had crying fits all the time and was afraid to go to sleep at night. Abuela said I had a case of *susto*, which means "scared" in Spanish. She told me that susto happened when the soul left the body 'cause of some awful event and it was too darned scared to come back. That talk about souls was downright confusing to me back then, and even now I wasn't so clear on what it all meant. I wondered where the soul went when it got scared. Did it hide under the covers like I did?

What I was certain of was that Abuela cured me right good by performing a limpia on me. It mighta sounded like mumbo jumbo and all, but everybody in town knew that Abuela's healing powers were real and they worked. And even though Mama had no use for Abuela's kinda medicine, I was in such a bad way after Daddy died that she let Abuela help me.

I was real little then, but I still remember pretty well most of what she did for me. Abuela had me lie down in my bed to do the limpia. It was a lot like what Pappy told me she'd done to heal him when he took sick. First thing, she swept a raw egg over my body, making crosses with it, going from my head to my feet. At the same time, she recited some gobbledygook from the Bible that I didn't know by heart. Abuela said that running the egg over me was to draw out the toxins and the bad energy and make it safe for my soul to return. Then she cracked the egg open and dropped it into a jar of water. Somehow, she read what was troubling me from how the egg shaped itself after it got plunked in the water. There weren't ABCs or nothing in the eggy water, or else I woulda known how to read the cracked egg too. It had something to do with how cloudy the white part of the egg was.

Next thing she did to heal me was put the jar with the egg under my bed, under the place where my head was. The next morning, there was an awful smell in my room. It was 'cause Abuela was burning some dried plants in a clay dish. For a whole lotta days after that, she made me drink some special teas that dang near made me puke. But it all worked, 'cause I finally stopped crying, and my troubles sleeping were over.

Pappy nudged me, reminding me that we were in church. Somehow, he could always tell when my head was somewhere far away.

Reverend Crawford was ending his sermon: "As we embark on the week ahead, let us feel the presence of the Lord with us in all that we do." The whole congregation roared, "Amen." I said a loud amen myself, grateful it was finally over so me and Paul could hike to the crater. We were trying to make a habit of going there every Sunday after church. Church for me, that is. I had a hankering to ask Paul about his being a Jew and what they believed in and stuff, especially on account of what the reverend had said about the Jews betraying Jesus and all. I just had to catch him when he didn't have his *No Trespassing* sign up.

It was Paul's turn to bring along food. My mouth was watering for his bubby's little meat pastries. I fetched Paul from his noisy house, and we set off on our hike. We walked along quiet as a coupla dead beetles. I was fixing to start asking my questions when all of a sudden Paul grabbed my arm.

"What is that?" he asked in a panicked voice.

"I didn't hear nothin'," I said.

"Listen! Something in bush."

Sure enough, there was rustling coming from the nearby tarbush. In a flash, a critter about the size of a cat, with dark fur and a white stripe down its back, stopped not more than three feet in front of us.

"A skunk," I whispered. "Be quiet and stand still.

Don't want him mad at us." The critter just stared at us with his beady eyes, like we were trespassing on his property and he didn't like it none.

"That little guy. He cannot hurt us." Paul laughed and bent down for a closer look.

The skunk started stomping his front feet and raking the ground with his claws.

"Oh no. Oh no," I said and backed away slowly.

When the critter arched his back and hissed, I knew we were in big trouble.

"RUN!" I yelled. I took off, but I wasn't two hoots and a holler away when I stopped to look back to make sure Paul was following me. "Come on!" I waved him toward me. "Over here!"

Paul was still crouched down and reaching out to pet the skunk. But it turned around, raised its tail, and sprayed. Even from where I had gotten myself to, I sure as heck smelled it. But it hit Paul with full force since he was right in front of the critter. He stumbled like a blind man over to where I was, waving his hands in front of him. His eyes were redder than a raw steak, and tears were streaming down his cheeks.

"Pee-hew!" I held my nose. "Uck! That's stinkier than rotten meat!"

"*Chert poberi!* I not feel well, James. Ohhhh." Paul put his hands over his eyes. "Oy, my eyes, they have needles in them."

"Let's get home. Pappy will know what to do." I draped Paul's arm over my shoulder and practically dragged him all the way to my house. He was wobbling like he had drunk a gallon of giggle water. On the way, we had to stop a coupla times 'cause we both had to vomit.

"Hey, Paul, ya think maybe we're bein' punished on account of what we did to Virgil? You know, with the twig girdlers and all?" It even crossed my mind that maybe Virgil had sent that darn skunk after us somehow.

"Is not possible," he answered, groaning at the same time. "What we did to Virgil, he deserve."

"But the reverend's always preachin' about doin' unto others as you would have 'em do unto you. Maybe we were askin' for it is all I'm sayin'."

"You not remember all those times Virgil bother you? Is more like he do unto you and do unto you and do unto you, until finally we do unto him." He moaned. "Are we almost there?"

When we got to my house, Pappy pinched his nose closed every time he got near us. "Gettin' the smell off you boys is gonna be like puttin' socks on a rooster," he said. He filled up the washbasin with tomato juice and made us bathe in it.

I reckoned that smelling like tomatoes was better than smelling like skunk. And I sure didn't want to have a bad smell about me when I went to school the next day. I didn't need to give Virgil and Margaret and the other kids one more reason to make fun of me. Most of all, I didn't want to give Fanny a reason to stay clear of me.

Chapter 17
Mama's Last Day in Jail

Come Monday morning, Paul and I barely smelled skunky anymore. And by some miracle, I survived that whole week of school without Virgil pounding on me. I avoided him as much as I could, skedaddling home the minute Miss Pritchert rang the school bell, keen to get through the week in one piece. I'd gotten Pappy to agree to take me to see Mama on Friday, on account of he'd just hired a part-time fry cook to spell him in the kitchen while we were away. I sure didn't wanna be visiting Mama at the end of the week with my face all bruised up, showing I'd been getting in fights.

Friday finally came around, and before Pappy and I left for the jailhouse, I fished the metal charm out from under my waist union suits in my bureau drawer and stuck it in my pocket. We were bumping along in the truck when Pappy sprung the bad news on me. "They're takin' your mama to the state hospital this weekend, probably tomorrow, so I was thinkin' you might like to have a little longer visit with her today."

My eyes welled up. I was nowhere near ready for her to go away so soon. We pulled up by the jail, and before he climbed outta the truck, Pappy squeezed my shoulder and said, "It'll be okay, Butch."

I wiped my eyes dry 'cause I didn't want Mama to catch me looking sad. When we went in, Deputy Fry brought Mama out from her cell. Pappy said his usual quick howdy to her and left to go wait in the truck. Mama and I dragged the two wobbly chairs away from the table and over to the side of the room where we could sit across from each other without a table separating us. Deputy Fry leaned against the wall nearby with his arms folded across his chest, eyeballing us.

Mama was smiling, and her eyes were sparkling. I crossed my fingers that that meant she wasn't gonna have to go to that hospital after all.

"You seem a whole lot better, Mama," I said. "So can you come home instead of going to that hospital?"

She grabbed ahold of both my hands. "I'm having one of my colorful days, honey. Even this jailhouse looks bright to me today. But just yesterday, I couldn't even get my head off the pillow. I need to have more of those good days instead of the dark ones. You understand me, James Aaron?"

"But if you come home, Pappy and me could help you. We could cheer up your spirits when they needed cheerin' up."

"I need more help than you or your pappy can give me, sweetie boy. There are gonna be special doctors at that hospital who know what to do for me." She squeezed my hands. "I promise I'll get myself all well, and then I'll come home and be a real good mama to you. But let's not talk about that. Let's talk about what kinda mischief you've been gettin' into lately."

Mama was acting so regular right then that I felt like spilling out to her every little thing that was on my mind. "I've been spendin' a lotta time with my friend Paul, Mama."

"He your best friend?" she asked.

"Yup. And now I know why he never has to go to church on Sundays." I looked over to make sure Deputy Fry wasn't listening to our conversation. He was busy exploring inside his nose with his pointer finger. "It's 'cause he's a Jew. And it don't really bother me. Did you know we don't have his kinda church here?"

"That's interesting. I wasn't aware there were any Jews in town, myself. And why would it bother you at all that he's a Jew anyhow?"

"Well, on account of the stuff folks say about 'em."

"What are you hearin'?" Mama asked.

"For starters, that the Jews killed Jesus Christ. And that they're moneygrubbin' people. Even Reverend Crawford says the Jews turned in Christ for thirty pieces of silver. And Margaret Bossco from school says she heard they have horns and that shows they're in cahoots with the devil."

"Honey, that's pure hogwash." Mama had that look she gets when she's tasted something awful and is searching for a place to spit it out. "Don't you go swallowin' stories that ignorant folks feed you about a people just 'cause they have some different beliefs than what you're used to."

"I figured it wasn't true, Mama. Especially the part about Jews havin' horns. Paul's got no horns."

"That's my boy. You gotta keep questionin' things and not go acceptin' everything you hear as gospel." She glanced over at Deputy Fry, who had switched from nose-picking to chewing on his lower lip and studying his fingernails. "So have you and Paul been stirrin' up any trouble?"

"We finally gave Virgil Jackson what for. We put some twig girdlers down his pants. You shoulda seen the dance he did. Please don't tell Pappy, though."

"Nah, your pappy don't need to know everything," Mama said. "Sounds like you and your friend Paul have things in common."

She was right about that. For starters, we were Virgil's favorite targets. But there was other stuff too, like how we both liked book reading and had both lost our daddies, and neither of us was too well liked at school. But I didn't figure how she knew any of that. She musta been referring to how both of us hated Virgil. Anyhow, I didn't bother asking her 'cause I had a mess of things I wanted to tell her before they took her far away and visiting was gonna be a whole lot harder.

"Oh, and Mama, I've been givin' some thought to what I might wanna do when I get a little older. I might wanna be a healer like Abuela. Or maybe even a doctor. Malvern thinks I'd have a real knack for it."

"I'm not real keen on you doing your abuela's kinda healin', but you pursuin' being a doctor, that's mighty fine," she said. "I'm so doggone proud of you. You sure got the brains for it. Your daddy coulda been a doctor, you know." She was looking toward the scratched-up wooden door that led outside the jailhouse, like she half expected my daddy to walk on through it.

"He always took real fine care of me when I was feelin' poorly," Mama went on. "Sometimes he went with your abuela a-callin' on sick people. And he loved pepperin' Doc Johnson with a million questions about every sorta medical problem."

I shoved my hand in my pocket and rubbed my fingers over the charm. I was fixing to pull it out and ask Mama about it when all of a sudden she burst out crying.

"I'm sorry for not bein' a good mama to you, James. And I'm sorry I'm leavin' you." She covered her face with her hands, and I saw that her nails were all bitten down. Then she reached out and pulled me to her and hugged me so tight that I was having trouble breathing. It surprised me on account of she wasn't one to do much hugging. My eyes got full.

Deputy Fry stepped over to us and said, "Let go of the boy," like he thought Mama was gonna squeeze the life outta me or something.

She dropped her arms for a second and stared down Deputy Fry as if she was shooting bullets at him through her eyes. Tears were running down her cheeks. "Can't a mama hug her little boy goodbye?"

I left the charm in my pocket, and me and Mama went back to hugging, trying to pretend like Deputy Fry wasn't hovering over us. Right about then, the jailhouse door creaked open and Pappy stepped in.

"It's time we got back, James," he said in a quiet voice.

"Jeb, you take good care of my boy, you hear?" Mama told him. She was wiping her cheeks with the back of her hand.

"You take care of yourself, Lucinda May," he said. "And you get yourself better so you can come home." He sounded like he meant it, even though everybody knew Pappy wasn't too fond of Mama.

Deputy Fry took Mama by the arm and walked her back to her cell. As we were leaving, she called out, "Jeb, it's time to share some family history with the boy!"

I wanted to run back and ask Mama what she meant, but she was already gone. Pappy put his big hand on my back and steered me outside.

"What did Mama mean by that?" I asked as we got in the truck. "What family history?"

"We'll talk about it later," he answered. "I need thinkin' time right now."

Wringing any information outta Pappy was harder than shooting flies with a shotgun. The rest of the way back to the diner, the only things doing any talking were the tires hitting the bumpy road.

Chapter 18
Learnin' Some Things

Seeing as Pappy still wasn't willing to open his mouth none, the second we got back to Ridgely's, I asked him if I could go over to Paul's. I was in the mood to be around his noisy family. "I won't stay over there long, Pappy," I said. "I promise."

The sun was already sinking, but Pappy said yes. He probably didn't need me at the diner that night on account of the new fry cook was helping him out. Anyhow, he was probably happy to get rid of me so he could dodge any more questions from me. I hurried over to Paul's, where I could count on there being plenty of talking.

Most of the time, Paul's house was as noisy as a brood of cackling hens, and I could hear the commotion before I even went inside. But this time when I knocked, I didn't hear a sound. I reckoned nobody was home, but I couldn't figure out where in tarnation everybody woulda gone on a Friday night. I knocked again, a little louder. I was fixing to leave when the door creaked open real slowly and only halfway. Paul peeked out, looking surprised to see me. He was wearing one of those big hats with the brim like he wore the time I was there for their Jewish New Year's.

I stole a look inside through the half-open door. I could see Paul's family all standing at one end of the long dinner table, crowded around a pair of silver candlesticks with lit candles in them.

Paul opened the door all the way. His mama, his sister, his stepfather, Uncle Ruvin, Aunt Yetta, and Bubby were all staring hard at me, as if I was the sheriff come to arrest them or something. I stood still as a post in the front doorway, feeling like I had barged in on something real private and that I had no business being there.

"Sorry, Paul. I didn't mean to bother you," I said. "I better go."

"No, no," he said. "Is no bother." Paul looked over at his mama and said something to her in what I guessed was Russian. She nodded to him. "Come in. I invite you to eat dinner with us," Paul said, grabbing my arm and pulling me over to where the candles were flickering.

I wanted to run outta there, but then Paul's mama said, "Velcome, James," trying out her English for my benefit. As usual, she didn't smile. But she spoke in a real friendly way, like her words were doing the smiling for her.

Samuel and Ruvin were wearing those same tall, furry hats they'd had on for their New Year's dinner. Samuel raised a silver cup sorta like the one Reverend Crawford used in church, and together they all muttered something in their language. Watching them pass the cup from one to the next, with each person taking a sip, I felt like I was witnessing some secret ritual that maybe I shouldn't be seeing.

Before she took a drink, Frieda handed me the cup. "Sip, James," she said.

I didn't know what was hiding in that cup, so I only pretended to drink. When I brought it up to my lips, I got enough of a whiff to know it was wine. I didn't have any fond feelings for the drink after seeing what it did to my mama. I got to wondering, though, how Paul's family got ahold of the stuff, seeing as it was illegal and all. Maybe they got it the same way my mama did—from the bootleggers.

In the middle of the table, there was a plate covered with an embroidered cloth. Samuel lifted the cloth. Under it was a loaf of bread that was braided just like the hair of some of the girls in our class. Paul's family said some more words in that throat-clearing language, and then Ruvin broke off small pieces of bread and passed them around. I got a soft piece from the inside of the loaf. Just then, I heard Virgil's voice in my head—when he was going on in school one time about how the Jews killed Christian children so's they could use their blood in some special bread they baked. 'Course, there couldn't have been an ounce of truth to it if Virgil said it. Besides, Paul's family wouldn't do something like that. But I couldn't kick the story outta my head, so just in case, I didn't eat the bread. I squished it up and shoved it in my pocket, hoping nobody saw me do it.

Then Paul's stepfather held his hands like two hats over Paul's and Frieda's heads and said a bunch more words. At the end, everybody started hugging and kissing and repeating the same couple of words to one another.

"What's going on?" I whispered to Paul.

"It's our—how you say it?—blessings? For Shabbas."

"Shabbas?" I asked.

"Is what we call the Sabbath."

"But the Sabbath isn't until Sunday—day after tomorrow," I whispered.

"Shabbas begins for Jewish people on sundown Friday."

"Then when does it end?" I asked him. I sure woulda hated having to sit in church and do all that praying and stuff from Friday night all the way through Sunday.

"When sun goes down on Saturday," Paul said.

"Please, you sit," Paul's mama told me, pointing to a chair at the table.

Maybe I shoulda been thinking about getting back to Pappy—I hadn't figured on being gone for dinner—but the cooking smells were too tempting to pass up.

"Thank you kindly, ma'am," I said. I still sorta felt like an intruder, barging in on them, but at the same time, it felt good being with Paul's family at their Sabbath table. Like somehow I belonged.

Paul and I sat next to each other. Frieda set out a

plate and utensils at my place. While we were wait-ing for the food, I asked Paul, "What's that language you were all mumblin'?"

"We say the prayers in Hebrew. It is our ancient language."

"It sounds different from the Russian I hear your family speakin'," I said.

"I not tell you this before, James, but we are not speaking Russian in our house. Remember that time at crater when you asked me to teach you Russian?"

"Yeah, and you said no, but you didn't explain why not," I said.

"Is because I not know very much Russian." Paul's leg was bouncing under the table. "Russian government did not allow my Jewish school in Ukraine to teach us Russian. But I still learned some curses in that language."

"Then what are you and your family speakin'?" I asked.

"Is called Yiddish, special language of Jewish people."

Paul's mama and his aunt Yetta came outta the kitchen and set down steaming bowls of chicken soup with tiny, thin noodles. When I finished my soup,

I tried to bring my empty bowl into the kitchen, but Frieda stopped me.

"That's my job," she said and went around the table collecting the empty bowls. I could see that in Paul's house, the women and girls took care of all the meals, and the men had nothing to do with it. That sure was different than the way things were with me and Pappy.

Then Frieda and her mama and aunt served us roasted meat swimming in its juice, broiled potatoes, and beet pickles. I ate every bite, cleaning my plate, like Mama taught me to do. I didn't do it just to be polite. The food was as tasty as Pappy's Ridgely burgers. But I shoulda known better than to eat those pickles on account of they made my tongue all bumpy.

"I'm stuffed," I told Paul. I could feel my belly pressing against the top button of my britches.

"No room for dessert? Bubby baked *putterbulkies*."

"Putter whats?"

Paul pointed to the plate of cinnamon rolls his mama was putting on the table. Something with a name that funny had to be worth trying, so I found a little room in my belly for a putterbulkie. It was sure worth overstuffing myself for.

After the food and dishes were cleared away, the men started up doing some lively singing and tapping on the table while they sang.

"What's goin' on now?" I asked Paul.

"They are singing special blessings for after the Shabbas meal."

Paul joined in the singing too. I didn't understand none of it, so I started looking around the room. I caught sight of that candlestick I'd seen before at his house, the one with spaces for a bunch of candles that was sitting on a shelf in the bookcase over in the corner. I started thinking real hard about where else I'd seen something like it. Then I remembered. Under the table, I pulled the charm outta my pocket. My eyes were darting back and forth between the candlestick and the charm in my hand. I brought the charm up close to my eyes so I could examine the picture on it of the teeny-tiny candlestick with seven branches.

"What you have there, James?" Paul whispered.

"Dunno. Maybe *you* can tell *me*," I whispered back and pointed to the bookcase. "You got somethin' right over there that looks like the raised picture on my charm."

He took the charm from me and crinkled up his

nose while he eyeballed it. That's how he looked when he was puzzling over something. "From where you get this?" he asked.

"My abuela—my grandmother—gave it to me just before she passed. She told me to keep it to myself, so I shouldn't be showing you," I said.

I pointed again to the candlestick on the bookshelf. "You told me before that your mama brought that here from your country. But what's it for?"

"Is called a menorah, and we light it on our holiday of Chanukah," Paul said.

Learning that my charm from Abuela had some kinda Jewish symbol on it left me more confused than ever.

"Did she wear around her neck? There is place for putting chain on the end," Paul said. "From where did your grandmother get it?"

"Fact is, I never saw it on her or anywhere else 'fore she slipped it into my hand the day she died," I answered. "There's some writin' on it. Can you make out what it says?"

Paul looked closely at it again. "Samuel would know," he said. "I see it is in Hebrew language. I know some, but I cannot read this."

"Hebrew—like you were recitin' your prayers in?

Like from the Bible? Why do ya reckon my abuela would have something with Hebrew on it?" I was getting more confused by the minute.

Paul shrugged. "I do not know. Is okay if I show Samuel?"

"Dang, I wasn't supposed to let anyone see it. But I guess the cat's outta the bag now," I said. All I could think about then was that I might be getting close to learning what the charm meant.

"What cat? And bag? What do you mean?" Paul asked.

"Never mind," I said. "Go ahead and show Samuel."

Paul said something to Samuel and passed the charm over to him. Samuel studied it for a while, and pretty soon everyone gathered around him to see what he was looking at. They were all talking at once and getting excited, as if they had just discovered a gusher of black gold underground.

"What are they carryin' on about, Paul?"

"They say this object is very, very old. And it has words to our most important prayer, *Shema Yisrael*. It means we believe in one God. My family wants to know why your grandmother had this, James."

"I couldn't tell you, Paul, but I mean to find

out. I'm hoping my pappy will know," I said. Soon as I mentioned Pappy, I remembered that I hadn't told him I wasn't coming back to the diner for dinner.

"I gotta skedaddle. My pappy will be gettin' worried. I'll see ya." I took the charm back, thanked Paul's family, and said my goodbyes.

Heading home, I did a fair share of stumbling on account of I had a hard time seeing my way in the dark. By the time I got to the diner, the CLOSED sign was hanging on the door and Pappy was inside scrubbing the counters.

"What happened to you?" Pappy snapped at me. "You were goin' over to your friend's for a quick visit, so you said, and look what time it is now. Help me sweep these floors so we can go home and get some sleep."

All I wanted to do was get some answers about the charm, but I knew I had to wait till Pappy simmered down. So I swept up the crumbs and whatever else was dirtying up the floor. While I swept, I thought about how Abuela had told me not to tell anyone about the charm. I wondered if she woulda been real disappointed in me for showing Paul's family. And I couldn't figure how I was gonna get any answers from Pappy without showing him the charm too. I decided that Abuela probably didn't mean for me to keep it secret from Pappy on account of he was probably the only one who could tell me anything about it.

Soon as I finished sweeping and put the broom away, I couldn't wait any longer. "I got somethin' to show you," I said to Pappy. I pulled the charm outta my pocket and held it up.

Pappy fixed his eyes hard on it. "Where'd you get that, James?" It seemed like forever that he was staring at it without blinking. To my surprise, his eyes started watering up.

"From Abuela. Day she passed," I said, almost in a whisper.

"You been holdin' on to that since your abuela passed and never thought to show it to me?" Pappy asked. His voice sounded more like he was puzzling over it than that he was mad at me for keeping it from him.

"She told me not to tell anyone about it. And I kept my word. Up till today, that is. But I just gotta know what this thing is and why Abuela gave it to me."

Pappy let out a huge sigh. "James, that's a chat

we need to have, but it's . . . somewhat complicated. No time to get into it now, given the lateness of the hour. Don't forget, we've gotta get up early in the mornin' for the breakfast crowd."

"Can't you just tell me what it is now?" I wasn't gonna let Pappy put out his *No Trespassing* sign this time.

Pappy gave me a hard look. "Well, the short answer is that it's a very old amulet that your abuela kept hidden in a drawer, and I darn near forgot it even existed."

"What's an amulet?" I asked.

"It's somethin' that protects against evil. A bit like a rabbit's foot."

"But why'd Abuela have an amulet with a Hebrew prayer on it, and why'd she give it to me?"

"How do you know that's what the writing is?" Pappy asked.

"From Paul's family," I said, hoping Pappy wouldn't be too sore at me for showing them.

"I see," Pappy said. "Let's get somethin' straight before we talk any more about it. Whatever I tell you is gonna have to stay just between us."

"Okay, but when are you gonna answer my questions?"

"How about we finish cleanin' up here and get ourselves home? And tomorrow, after the breakfast crowd thins out, we'll come back to the house and have ourselves a sit-down. I'm gonna show you somethin' that'll hopefully make things as clear as runnin' water for you."

Chapter 19
Gettin' at the Truth

I stayed awake forever that night, puzzling over what the charm meant and wondering what Pappy could possibly show me that'd explain everything. But I couldn't find any answers hiding in the nooks and crannies of my head. To help me doze off, I tried counting sheep, picturing them wandering one by one over a grassy hill. But I only made it to fifty before a pack of wolves came along, cornered the sheep, and started closing in on them, baring their teeth and growling.

The next morning, Pappy had to shake me awake. I had a mighty hard time dragging myself outta bed, but he needed my help at the diner on account of the townsfolk were keen on taking their families to Ridgely's on Saturday mornings for his famous corn cake pancakes with spiced apples on top. I pulled on my overalls and checked to make sure I had a bandanna in my pocket. It was something Abuela had insisted I keep with me all the time. "Just in case a West Texas sandstorm decides to pay us a visit," she'd said. I picked up my charm, rubbed it between my fingers for luck, and stuck that in my pocket too.

The whole time I was helping, I kept wishing the diners would gobble up their food and skedaddle. Finally, the last customer left, so Pappy and I went back to the house for our talk. He told me to sit on the sofa while he fetched something from his bedroom. What he came back with was wrapped in an embroidered cloth. He unwrapped it carefully, and I saw it was a book. After brushing some dust off the cover, he handed it over to me real gently, like he was afraid the book was gonna fall apart. It looked like it was darn near a million years old.

"James, if you want to know about your abuela, for starters, have a look through this here Bible. It's been in her family for centuries. I reckon Marlena . . ." He choked up a little saying Abuela's name before he went on. "She was waiting until you were a bit older to share this with you, when you'd be better able to understand what it meant. But seeing as she gave you that amulet and you're asking so many questions, I think if she were still alive, she'd agree that now's the proper time." Pappy's joints creaked like an old door as he sat down in his rocking chair. He was sucking in his lips—something he did when he was concentrating hard.

I looked at the Bible in my lap. The cover was the color of pecans, and in gold letters it said *Sagrada Biblia*, which I suspected was Spanish for something like Holy Bible. I laid my hand on it and felt how brittle the leather was from being so worn.

The Bible's pages were thin and crinkly. I was almost too afraid to turn them 'cause I knew I was holding something so ancient that it was likely to crumble into nothing. But I was anxious to learn what secrets it was hiding, so I opened the book as slowly and carefully as I could.

"I can't read this, Pappy. Is it all in Spanish or what?"

Pappy was leaning back in the rocker with his eyes closed. "Turn to the back, to the endpaper," he said. "You'll find something you can read."

On the inside of the back cover, there was some sorta diagram with horizontal lines that had names and dates written across them. And those lines had short lines growing down from them like the roots of a turnip. I squinted to read the teensy-weensy handwritten names and saw that they weren't like any names I'd heard around Odessa. At the very top of the page, it said *Abran de Gerondi* and *Fermoza, fija de Josef.* Almost every line of names running down the page was written in different handwriting.

There was a surprise waiting for me near the bottom, though—my grandparents' names: *Marlena Olivera* and *Jeb Ridgely.* From their names, there was a short line connecting them to my mama's and daddy's names right below. And what I saw at the very bottom of the page, right underneath my mama and daddy, made my heart pound faster than a train speeding down the tracks. It was my own name: *James Aaron Ridgely.* Next to our names were our birth dates and, in the case of my daddy, the date he died. Abuela's name was missing the date of her death.

Seeing myself and the names of my kin on this map of names in the back of a dusty old Bible didn't answer my questions none. It just made new ones crop up.

"Who are all these people, and why are our names in here too?" I asked, pointing to the open book on my lap.

Pappy blinked his eyes open and leaned forward to see what I was pointing at.

"That there is a family tree. Those are names of your abuela's ancestors going way back through the generations."

"*Abran de Gerona* and *Fermoza, fija de Josef.* They're Mexican names, right?" I asked. "Are they Abuela's people from Mexico?"

"Before I get into that, I want to remind you again that what we talk about here is nobody's business but ours. It goes nowhere. Got it?"

My mouth said yes, but in my head, I was thinking that I was more than likely gonna share anything interesting I learned with Paul. And knowing me and Paul had a pact, I was certain that whatever stuff I told him at the crater wasn't going nowhere else.

"Truth is, those are the names of her family in Spain," he said.

"I'm not following, Pappy. Abuela came here from Mexico with her parents. That's what she told me."

Pappy got up from the rocking chair and came over to sit next to me on the sofa.

"Yeah, it's true your abuela came here from Mexico with her family. But way, way back—five hundred years ago or so—your abuela's grandparents'

grandparents, or maybe even more generations back than that, hailed from Spain."

Most of the time Pappy didn't let people get too near him, physically or otherwise, but he was sitting so close to me on the sofa that our elbows were rubbing against each other.

"Now, I don't claim to have too many of the details, mind you, and everything I'm telling you comes secondhand—from your abuela. And she didn't confide any of this in me until long after we got hitched and your daddy was born."

"Why didn't she ever tell *me* her family came from Spain? And who cares anyhow whether they came from Spain or Mexico? What's the difference?"

"Hold on now. I'm gettin' to that." Pappy pointed to the writing in the Bible. "So this family tree, it traces your abuela's ancestors all the way back to the 1400s, to this couple at the very top—Abran de Gerondi and Fermoza, fija de Josef. Back in 1492 in Spain . . ."

I blurted out, "*Columbus sailed the ocean blue. He had three ships and left from Spain. He sailed through sunshine, wind, and rain.*" I was showing off that I knew my history. "Did Abuela's family came over on Columbus's ship?" I was fixing to be mighty proud, picturing myself bragging to the kids at school about how my relations sailed to America on the *Santa Maria*.

"That's not how it was. Somethin' else happened in 1492. The king and queen of Spain kicked out all the Jews."

"Why'd they do that, Pappy?"

"Beats me, Butch. All I know is that the royal couple was Catholic, and they got it in their heads to hate the Jews 'cause they had some different beliefs."

"I don't understand what any of that has to do with me," I said, "except that you're sayin' some of my ancestors came from Spain."

"We're gettin' to it. Don't get your britches in a wad. You've got about as much patience as your mama, Butch." With his long, bony finger, he underlined the names at the top of the page. "This Abran and Fermoza, they were Jewish."

I got a funny feeling in my gut. "What're you gettin' at, Pappy? Are you sayin' Abuela was Jewish? She couldn'ta been. She went to the Catholic church every Sunday, and she used to take me with her."

"What I'm sayin' is that your abuela's ancestors didn't start out as Catholics. Accordin' to the stories passed down to your abuela, they had a heck of a choice if they wanted to stay in Spain. If they didn't want to be burned at the stake, they had to agree to be baptized as Christians. The thing is, some acted like Catholics on the outside but kept practicin' their Jewish ways in secret. And apparently, doin' that was real dangerous."

"What woulda happened to 'em if they got caught?" I asked.

"From what I heard tell, they woulda been thrown in a dark dungeon and tortured and maybe even been burned to death."

I winced. "Did that happen to anybody in Abuela's family?"

"Mighta. But somehow, somewhere down the line, some of Abuela's kin escaped Spain. Eventually, they crossed the ocean and settled in Mexico, and they brought this Bible with 'em." He traced a line from Abran and Fermoza all the way down to my name at the very bottom of the page.

My heart was pumping like I'd just finished running a hundred-yard dash. "You mean I got Jewish blood in me, Pappy?"

"It seems you do. At least a little bit."

"But we go to church and all. Always have. I can't be Jewish. I don't know nothin' about bein' Jewish, except maybe some stuff I saw Paul's family doin'."

"Like you said yourself, your abuela went to church too. She was reared Catholic. That's what she knew, exceptin' that it seems some Jewish rituals were quietly passed down in her family over the centuries. So just like her, you've got centuries of Jewish blood runnin' through you. Baptized or not, it's in you."

"Why didn't Abuela ever tell me this herself?"

"She was waitin' till she thought you were old enough and could be trusted to understand and be able to keep it to yourself. She a-feared that folks would treat you badly if they found out. You oughtta be aware, Butch, that there are folks out there who don't like Jews none." Pappy took the Bible from me, closed it gently, and smoothed his hand over the worn cover.

"Your grandmother was just trying to protect you, that's all. It seems every generation of her family had to hide being Jewish just so's they could stay alive—or at least get by without anybody botherin' them. But this don't change who you are, James." Pappy waved his long pointer finger at me.

I couldn't help thinking that he was dead wrong—that it changed a whole lot about who I was. I wasn't sure how yet, but I knew that it did. Then I understood why Mama had said that Paul and I had things in common. She musta known about my Jewish ancestors.

"Why didn't Mama tell me any of this?" I asked.

"Your mama knew it wasn't her story to tell. And your abuela had asked her not to say anything to you about it. Besides, your mama never saw this Bible, and she didn't know all the history."

I wished everybody hadn't decided they needed to keep this big secret from me. "Can I look through the Bible a little more?" I asked.

Pappy nodded and handed it back to me. "Take your time."

When I flipped to the pasted-down endpaper to take another look at the family tree, something caught my eye on the back of the page facing it. There was some tiny handwriting barely peeking out along the hinge of the spine. It wasn't the same sorta writing that was in the rest of the Bible, but the strange handwriting with its straight lines did look kinda familiar. I peered real closely at it and then dug the charm outta my pocket. My eyes traveled back and forth between the writing in the Bible and the even tinier writing on the charm. It sure did look like the same language, even though the letters didn't look exactly the same on both. I knew from Paul that it was Hebrew.

Things were starting to get a little less muddy. Between the charm and the Bible with my name in it and the Hebrew writing, I felt like Abuela was sending me a message from the grave, trying to tell me that I was somebody different than I'd thought I was. And I got to wondering, too, if this news about my family's past could have something to do with me finding my purpose. Even though the one person who coulda helped me figure that out was gone, maybe she was still speaking to me in a way. I needed to find out what those handwritten words hiding in the back of the Bible said.

"Pappy, ya think I could take this Bible over to Paul's? I'll be mighty careful with it."

"Now, why would you want to go and do that?"

"I think his stepfather might be able to translate somethin' written in here," I said. I held up the charm. "Paul's a Jew, you know."

"Yeah, I suspected as much," he said. "Even so, it's still nobody's business that you've got some Jewish in you, so let's just keep it between us, you hear?"

"I gotta tell Paul. He's the only one, I swear." Pappy and me were still sitting so close to each other that our arms were touching.

"I'm not keen on you tellin' anybody. It's nothin' to be ashamed of, mind you, but I'm just trying to protect you like your abuela woulda wanted me to. Plenty of people in this town might not think too kindly of you if word got out."

"People don't think too kindly of our family anyhow. And besides, Paul doesn't have to hide that he's Jewish. So how come I have to?"

"I reckon Paul and his family don't have much choice in the matter. Everybody knows they're Jewish. But nobody knows about this long-hidden, small part of you, and nobody needs to either," Pappy said. "I don't want you to go invitin' trouble."

"What kinda trouble would I be invitin' on account of people knowin' I had some Jewish ancestors?" I asked. I didn't get why Pappy was fretting so much. It's not like Paul's family had anything to fear in our country just 'cause they were Jewish, so far as I could tell.

"The whole reason Paul's family came here was 'cause it's safe for them here," I explained. "They left Ukraine on account of it was bad for Jews there."

"I got no doubt that your friend Paul's family is better off here than where they came from. But they've still gotta sleep with one eye open, seeing as there are folks right here in Texas who don't like Jews none and are keen on chasin' 'em out. For one thing, the Ku Klux Klan has been parading down Main Streets of our towns for years, stirring up trouble for Jews, people with darker skin, and anybody else who doesn't look like them or holds some different beliefs." Pappy turned his head and made a spitting sound like he was getting rid of a bad taste in his mouth. "Those yellow-bellied Klan cowards hide their faces under white pointy hoods while they go around burnin' crosses on people's yards and committin' violent acts."

I flashed to the time I heard Margaret bragging at school about how her daddy was some kinda big shot in the Klan. But I'd had no inkling of what they were about.

"Now you understand why I don't want your news gettin' out?"

"Don't worry, Pappy. I'm not plannin' to share this with anybody but Paul."

Pappy fixed me a worried look. "Well . . . it might help you to have somebody to talk to about it—somebody who can understand," he said. "You can tell Paul only if you're certain he can keep it to himself and not go blabbin' it to anybody else."

"I promise he won't spill the beans," I said, crossing my heart. "Can I bring the Bible over to his house?"

"I don't think it's a smart idea to take it anywhere. It's awfully old and fragile, and it's traveled through the centuries."

"Please, Pappy," I begged.

He stroked his bushy beard and peered at me for a spell. I had a feeling he was thinking about whether Abuela woulda been pleased or riled if I took the Bible over there.

"Well, if you promise not to let anybody but Paul's stepfather handle it and you keep it wrapped in the cloth the rest of the time, I suppose you can take it. But you gotta bring it back the minute you get that translation."

Chapter 20
Sharin' Stuff

The next day, before I could share my big news with Paul, I had to sit through Sunday church services. I caught Fanny's eye when we walked in, and she waved howdy. It gave me a warm feeling inside. Me and Pappy scooted along the pew she was sitting at the other end of. I wondered what she'd make of me being a little Jewish, especially seeing as how she was so devoted to the church. I supposed it didn't matter none 'cause she wasn't gonna ever find out. I kept stealing looks at her through the whole service, but every time I turned my head in her direction, Pappy poked me in the ribs. The most entertaining thing that morning was watching Fanny dozing off during her father's sermon. Her head bobbing up and down was a sight to see.

My ears perked up, though, when the reverend started talking about Paul the Apostle. I paid attention, figuring maybe he'd have something to say that I could share with Paul about his namesake.

Reverend Crawford bellowed, "My friends, let us pay heed to the words of Paul the Apostle, who said that in times of transition, we should *encourage one another*. Did he say we should *comfort* one another? No, instead he chose the word 'encourage,' I believe, because it means *to put courage into*."

Thanks to the reverend, I was gonna have a whole new way of looking at the word *encourage* whenever I'd see it in one of my books.

The reverend went on, "Paul tells us that in troubled times, especially in the face of death, we need the *courage* to keep moving forward even when the way is cloudy or sad or uncertain."

I sure woulda found that advice helpful if the reverend had shared it with me after my abuela's passing. Paul the Apostle sounded like a right smart fella. I figured my friend Paul would be glad to know that he chose a pretty good name for himself.

As soon as we finished singing the closing hymn, I raced home to grab the Bible and my knapsack with the food in it. Instead of running, I did some fast walking over to Paul's. Carrying the Bible, I was afraid that if I ran, I might trip and drop it. I sure was excited to show it to Paul—and to tell him about me having some Jewish ancestors. But I was planning to save that part of the story till we got to the crater.

First thing when Paul opened the door, I asked for his stepfather, so Paul invited me in. Samuel was sitting cross-legged on top of his worktable. His glasses were perched on the tip of his nose, and he was pulling a needle and thread through a pair of trousers. I set the Bible on the dining table and real carefully unwrapped the cloth around it. Samuel climbed off his worktable and stood next to me. I opened the Bible to the back and pointed to the tiny handwriting in the margin that I thought was Hebrew.

"Do you know what it says?" I asked Samuel.

He brought the book up close to his eyes and turned it sideways. He said some words to Paul in their language, and I gave Paul a questioning look.

"Samuel say this is our blessing for sick person," Paul explained. "It begins like this: *May he who blessed our fathers, Abraham, Isaac, and Jacob, bless and heal those who are ill.*"

I'd heard those words before. When Abuela was doing her healing and let me tag along, she'd say that same blessing and stick in the name of the sick person she was working on. It got me to wondering if reciting that blessing maybe coulda been one of those Jewish practices her people used to do in secret.

I pulled the amulet outta my pocket and held it up. "So the blessing on here is different than the one in that Bible?" I asked.

Samuel peeked at me over his eyeglasses and nodded.

"Your charm has the Shema on it—is the one I told you about before that means we believe in one God," Paul explained. "And in your book is the blessing for healing."

I shook my head, trying to make the pieces of information I was gathering fit together like puzzle pieces in my mind, to get them all to make one picture that made sense.

"You okay, James?" Paul asked. He was looking over my shoulder at the Bible. "Why do you have this book? In what language are the words?"

"It's a real old Bible. It was my abuela's, and I think it's mostly in Spanish. But how 'bout I tell you everything when we get to the crater?" I said, gently rewrapping the cloth around the Bible. "Can I leave this here and pick it up when we get back?"

"Sure," Paul said, and he set it on a high shelf on the bookcase, one that I couldn't even reach on my tiptoes. I reckoned he understood that the Bible needed to be put in a safe place.

We took off on our regular hike. Lucky for us, the weather was finally cooling down, making the walking easier. Even though I was bursting to share my news with Paul, I held it in. After all, I thought, if my abuela and her family from long ago coulda hidden their being Jewish all those years, it should be easy as pie for me to keep it secret for as long as it took to get to the crater. I started thinking about what woulda happened to my ancestors in Spain if someone had discovered they were sticking with some of their Jewish ways. Picturing them being burned at the stake made me shiver.

When we finally reached the crater, Paul and I plopped down in the dirt. We sat on the rim with our legs dangling over the edge.

"I got some mighty big news to share with you, Paul. And you gotta *swear to God, hope to die, stick a needle in your eye* that you won't tell anybody what I'm about to tell you."

"We have a deal, right? I not forget that what you tell me stays at crater, like always."

"Here goes. I'm a Jew, like you."

"No, you are not, James." Paul chuckled. "Is not possible. You go to church. You eat ham sandwiches. Your family is not Jewish."

I took the amulet from my pocket and waved it in front of him. "My grandmother put this in my hand 'fore she died on account of she wanted me to know that she was a Jew, and that meant I was too, at least part."

"I cannot believe it. You do not seem Jewish at all."

"That's because I don't know the first thing about bein' Jewish. I've only heard people say bad stuff about Jews. Even the reverend says the Jews killed our Savior."

Paul spit in the dirt. "You think these things are true?" he said.

"No. My mama says it's all a lot a hogwash and I shouldn't go believin' any of it."

"Your mama is right," Paul said. "I think she would agree with Uncle Ruvin. He always says to me, 'Ignorant people say ignorant things. Even in America.'"

We stopped talking and just kept swinging our legs and staring down into the crater. The air was still, and it was so doggone quiet that you coulda heard a parade of ants marching. Suddenly, a hawk started screeching. We both looked up, and I wondered if it was the same hawk we saw circling overhead the last time we were there. Maybe it was Abuela's spirit, and it made sense that it showed up right when I was in the middle of sharing our secret with Paul.

"Anyway," Paul said, "you are lucky to be in America, where no one even knows you are Jewish. And even if someone knows, I think, is better to be Jewish here. Like I tell you before, Russia is not good place for Jews."

Paul balled up his fists and stared into the distance so long without blinking that his eyes musta been stinging. Since I had just shared a giant secret with him, I decided to finally ask the question I'd been hankering to ask for a while but never did on account of I didn't want to cross Paul's *No Trespassing* sign.

"What happened to your daddy anyway? Did it have somethin' to do with his being a Jew?"

"I will tell you," Paul said, even though he still had a faraway look. "Russian peasants attacked the *shtetl*—the village—where my *tateh*—my father— went to live."

"Why'd they do that?" I asked.

"Because it was village of Jews, and the Russian government stirred up the peasants to hate the Jews."

"Didn't y'all live there together—you and your mama and Frieda?"

"No, it was after my tateh moved outta our house."

"You mean y'all lived in a different house than your daddy? Why'd he move out?"

"Is complicated story. My tateh had a clothing factory, and he want to get business to make uniforms for all of Russian army, but they say because he is Jewish he cannot have that business. So he decide to become Christian so they will let him make uniforms, and that will earn much money for his company."

While he was telling his story, Paul's face got all scrunched up and splotchy red. "But my muter was very angry. She did not want him to change religion, so she forced him to leave our house. Later, Tateh was attacked where he was living."

"Were you with your tateh when they attacked?" I asked.

"No, but I wish I was. Maybe I could have done something. I was living with my muter. We only heard about it later."

"What happened?" I asked.

"The peasants, they move in a group from house to house, like many bees looking to sting. They broke into my tateh's house and . . ." Paul started taking quick, short breaths and clenched his fists like he was fixing to knock someone straight into next week. "They hurt him so badly, he not survive. Then they took all his clothes and dishes and everything he owned with them."

Paul's eyes watered up. I set my hand on his arm. "That's the worst thing I ever did hear, Paul." I wished I coulda found more comforting words for him. "Seems like your daddy was struck by lightnin' too, in a way." Only, the lightning that had struck Paul's daddy looked an awful lot like a bunch of vicious good-for-nothings, instead of a bolt from the sky that didn't go out looking for anybody. "So, did you come to America on account of what happened to your daddy?"

Paul's breathing slowed down. "That was part of the reason. But my muter was already married to Samuel by then. She was worried the Russians would take me away to be in army. They took Jewish boys as young as ten years old. The other soldiers not treat them well. They beat up the Jewish boys."

I stood up and looked around for a rock. I found a small one and hurled it into the crater. "That's for the soldiers who hurt the Jewish boys in the Russian army!" I yelled.

Paul got up too, threw a rock, and cried, "That is for the Russian peasants who killed my tateh!"

I took another turn. "That's for the lightnin' that killed my daddy!"

"And that is for all the people in Russian government who hate us!" Paul hollered, heaving a large rock.

I wound up my arm like a baseball player and pitched another rock. "And that's for the king and queen of Spain who kicked out the Jews!"

We each picked up one more stone. "For Virgil?" I asked, and Paul nodded.

"That's for Virgil Jackson!" we yelled together, throwing our rocks as far as we could.

All that throwing and yelling got us outta breath.

We stood there silent for a while. I think the rock throwing helped, but I was still looking for something to say to help ease Paul's sad feelings. Then I remembered the reverend's words.

"In church this morning, Reverend Crawford was talkin' about your namesake, Paul the Apostle.

Paul said that in the troubled times, we need to give each other courage, or something like that. I think you've already got a load a courage. I'd say you chose a good name for yourself, seeing as Paul shared some real wise words with us."

Paul sorta smiled. Then he said, "Let's go home, James."

When we got back to town, I said see ya later to Paul. Before he went his way and I went mine, he put his hand on my shoulder and said, "Now we are more alike than we thought."

Chapter 21
Virgil Troubles Again

Soon as I got back from our Sunday hike, Pappy asked in a friendly way, "What did your friend Paul have to say about your newly discovered family history?" But then he looked down at my hands and fixed me with a stare so hard it felt like his eyes were drilling holes right through me, and his voice turned angry. "Where's the Bible, James?"

I remembered leaving it at Paul's house, and my belly got tighter than a fist. I couldn't meet Pappy's eyes when I answered. "I'm truly sorry, Pappy. We went hikin' and I didn't wanna carry it with me, so's to keep it safe I left it at Paul's—all wrapped up in the cloth, mind you."

"I knew I shouldn'ta let you take it. You gotta be more responsible with things, James. I expect you to march back over there right now and collect that Bible, you hear? And I'm goin' with you, seein' as it's gettin' dark."

Pappy and I made our way over to Paul's house, but not without me tripping over rocks and getting my foot caught in a gopher hole, since there wasn't much of a moon to light the path. Paul's uncle Ruvin answered the door when we knocked. It was a good thing, too, 'cause he spoke the best English of the grown-ups in that house. I introduced him to Pappy, and they shook hands. I couldn't tell if Ruvin was happy to meet him or not. Like Pappy, he had a bushy mustache and beard that kept his mouth hidden and made it hard to tell what he was feeling.

"He is a good boy, your James," Ruvin said, patting me on the head. I crossed my fingers that him saying that would go toward lessening Pappy's disappointment in me.

"I'm right sorry to bother you. I know it's late, but I believe my grandson left a Bible here," Pappy said.

"Pinkus!" Ruvin called over his shoulder and then yelled something in their language.

Paul came to the door, carrying the Bible like

it was a bowl of hot soup. "Hello, Mr. Ridgely," he said and handed it to Pappy. "I am sorry we forget to get it after we hiked."

"Don't you worry none. It's not your concern, son," Pappy said. Then he nodded at Paul's uncle, and as we were leaving, he said to Paul, "Have James bring you by for dinner again real soon."

By the time we got home, my feet were mighty tuckered out from so much walking, and my head hurt from all the new thoughts and ideas whirling around inside it—and from disappointing Pappy so badly. So I told Pappy I was okay skipping supper and going straight to bed.

When I woke up the next morning, I told Pappy that I was feeling poorly and that I oughtta stay home. I wasn't keen on going to school for two big reasons. Somehow, I got it in my head that soon as I walked into the classroom, the kids would know I was hiding something. And I didn't want to be at school 'cause I knew Virgil was gonna be looking for a way to get his revenge on me and Paul for those twig girdlers.

I was still in bed when Pappy felt my forehead and asked me if anything hurt.

"Guess not," I said. There was no pulling the

wool over Pappy. It was the beginning of a new week, and he sure wasn't gonna let me skip school unless I had the plague.

The only thing wrong with me that Monday was that I knew I was different. But when I got to school, nobody was looking at me funny or paying me any heed. I guess I still looked exactly the same on the outside even if I was a little bit different now, a little bit Jewish, on the inside. I was still a skinny, shrimpy kid with brown hair, and eyes the green of a prickly pear cactus. Margaret poked fun at me as usual, calling me *pip-squeak* and *lightnin' boy*. And Fanny kept sharing her secret smiles with me. I gotta admit, my biggest worry was that Fanny, being the daughter of the reverend, wouldn't like me too much if she found out I wasn't Christian through and through.

Lunch recess came, and sure enough, I felt a push from behind that darn near knocked me on my knees.

"That's for them twig girdlers, and that's just for starters," Virgil snarled.

I turned around to face him, and he punched me in the stomach real hard before I had a chance to use my new blocking skills. I doubled over, and Virgil pushed me to the ground. Then he was on top of me. We rolled over and over, grappling while I tried to protect myself from his punches. I was tasting blood. A bunch of kids made a circle around us. There was a whole chorus of yelling, but I heard one voice in particular while I was getting clobbered.

"STOP IT! Get off of him, Virgil!" Fanny was screaming.

Paul was trying to pull Virgil off me, but Virgil kept hitting me.

Suddenly, Miss Pritchert was screaming, "Virgil, stop this instant! Get up, both of you, and follow me!" Virgil got off me, and Paul helped me up. I put my hand up to my aching face, and pretty quick it turned red with blood. While I stumbled over to Miss Pritchert, Virgil stayed back. I saw him looking at something on the ground and bending down for a second before he followed us.

With blood dripping from my nose, I dragged myself behind Miss Pritchert into the empty class-room, where she ordered me and Virgil to take our seats. We sat at our desks while she went through her supplies. She pulled out a cloth that maybe was white once upon a time.

"Virgil, go out to the pump, get this cloth wet, and come right back," she said.

He sure took his sweet time, probably hoping all my blood would drain outta me while he was gone. He finally came back in and handed the wet cloth to Miss Pritchert.

"Here, James—hold this on your nose and put some pressure on it. Now, care to tell me what this fight was all about?" She looked at me first.

"Yes ma'am," I said. "Virgil started the whole thing. He pushed me on the ground, then started punching me."

"Liar!" Virgil hollered. "He's just tryin' to get me in trouble. What really happened was he come up behind me when I wasn't lookin' and pushed me. Then his big dumb Russian friend held me down while James beat on me. James and his dopey friend are always doin' terrible things to me. Last week they put twig girdlers down my trousers. Got a temper like his mama, he does."

"Is this true, James?" Miss Pritchert asked.

"Not very much of it, ma'am," I said.

"What part of it would you say is true?"

"Well, I, uh, mighta shared some twig girdlers with him, but I swear that's all," I told her.

Virgil had a smirk on his face that I wanted to slap right off.

"Virgil, why were you hitting James?" Thank the Lord, Miss Pritchert was turning her attention to the real culprit.

"I was just defendin' myself. He started the whole thing. And I'm right sorry you had to be bothered with this, Miss Pritchert."

Virgil's voice was making my stomach turn, like the time I ate some bad meat.

I looked up and saw a bunch of faces peering in the schoolhouse window. Maybe the other kids were checking to see if I was still alive. Miss Pritchert waved her hand to shoo them away. "Y'all don't come back here till I ring the bell that recess is over," she said to them in her sternest voice. Then she turned back to me and Virgil. Some strands of her hair had already escaped from her bun and were hanging along the sides of her face. Usually, her hair didn't get like that till the end of the day.

"I want you boys to stay after school, and each of you must write on the chalkboard fifty times, 'I will not fight with my classmates.' You're just lucky I don't take a switch to the both of you. And James, I want you to concentrate on controlling your temper. There's a real strong tendency in your family that you need to overcome. As for you, Virgil, I suspect you don't have it so easy at home, but that doesn't give you the right to take it out on your classmates. Taunting and fighting are not going to make things better for you."

Then Miss Pritchert made us shake hands. The last thing I wanted to do was touch Virgil's grimy paw. And I know he wasn't too keen on shaking mine neither, so we did it real quick, barely letting our hands meet.

Miss Pritchert rang the outside bell to signal the end of lunch recess. I never even got to open my lunch pail on account of the fight. My belly was doing some right loud grumbling. When the other kids came back into the classroom, they gaped at me with wide eyes. I reckoned I looked pretty awful holding a bloody cloth on my nose. At least Paul stopped by my desk and asked if I was okay. And Fanny, looking real worried, even laid her hand on my arm when she passed by.

By the end of the school day, my hungry belly was making quite a ruckus. It was probably mad at me for starving it, but it was gonna have to wait. Virgil and I stayed after class to write our sentences on the blackboard, shooting daggers at each other with our eyes the whole time. Miss Pritchert sat at her desk, grading some papers while she kept an eagle eye on us.

Boy, was I gonna be in hot water with Pappy for getting to the diner so late. He was already not happy with me for forgetting to bring the Bible home. I practically ran the whole way to the diner— not just 'cause I was late, but also 'cause I didn't want to give Virgil a chance to practice more punching on me.

Pappy was standing by the grill when I got to Ridgely's. I could smell the burgers frying, which made my empty stomach growl even more.

"Pappy, I'm real sorry I'm late. Had to get some extra help from my teacher after school."

"Hmm. I guess Miss Pritchert's got a pretty powerful right hook, eh?"

I had plumb forgotten about my bloody nose, which had stopped gushing thanks to the pressure of the cloth. I musta been a sight, though—dried blood crusting around my nose and creeping down toward my mouth and spotting my white shirt.

I figured the faster I told my story, the more likely we'd get the whole incident over with in a flash. "Okay, so I got sandpapered by Virgil Jackson, and we had to stay after school and write sentences, which wasn't fair 'cause I didn't start nothin'. But Miss Pritchert didn't believe my side. I think she thinks I caught somethin' from Mama, like a fightin' disease. My nose is fine, though, so whatya need help with today?"

"Hold on there, James. What are we going to do about this problem with Virgil? It doesn't seem to be leavin' town." Pappy was mashing up taters in a giant pot while he kept an eye on the burgers.

"I'll try to stay outta his way," I said.

"How are you fixin' to do that?" Pappy said. "You've gotta see him every day in school. You're wastin' too much time being at the other end of Virgil's fist. I think it's time I go over and have me a chat with the boy's father."

"That's just gonna make Virgil madder. Let me handle this myself, Pappy."

"You're not to handle it with your fists, you hear me?" Pappy wagged his finger at me. "If Virgil cleans your plow again, I'm gonna have to step in, understand? Now I gotta get cookin'. We've got hungry customers. You go on and wash that blood off your face and scrub those hands real good."

I was glad to be done with that conversation. I went into the kitchen and cleaned myself off in the big basin and finally gobbled down the soggy sandwich from my lunch pail. I woulda rather had a Ridgely burger, but Pappy wasn't offering. Then I got to work washing off cabbages and peeling carrots. I was afraid my nose was swelling up, so I stopped working for a minute and went to the freezer to get myself a chunk of ice to wrap in a towel and hold on it. My smarting nose got me badly wishing Abuela were there to do some healing on me. Something besides just pressing ice on my injury. With my free hand, I fished into my pocket for the amulet, on account of I got some comfort from rubbing it. But all I pulled out was some dirt. When I found nothing in the other pocket either, my insides started twisting up.

I coulda sworn I'd taken the amulet outta these same britches the day before to show Paul when we were at the crater. I crossed all my fingers that I'd find it at home. I was praying that, on account of me being so beat after our hike and having to go all the way back to Paul's for the Bible, I'd taken the amulet outta my pocket before I conked out in my bed. And instead of putting it back in my pocket before going to school, I musta left it at home.

"I'll be back in a jiffy, Pappy," I said after I finished washing and peeling. "I gotta go fetch somethin' from home."

As soon as I got in the door, I raced to my room to look for the amulet. I held my breath while I opened the top drawer of my chest, where I usually kept it hidden, and fished around in my clothes. I couldn't find it, so I yanked open the other two drawers. My heart was beating faster than it shoulda been. The amulet wasn't in any of the drawers. The whole chest was about to pitch forward from the weight of the open drawers, so I closed them real fast. Maybe I shoulda just let myself get flattened. It woulda served me right for losing the most important thing I'd owned.

I had to find that amulet. Keeping it with me had made me feel like somehow Abuela was nearby.

When I got back to the diner, Pappy said, "Feelin' okay there, Butch? Your face is darn near as white as a picket fence."

I just shook my head. I couldn't look him in the eye. Then he saw my empty hands and asked, "Whatya get from the house?"

I fessed up and told him that I'd gone looking for the amulet. "I . . . uh . . . just left it somewhere, and

I'm gonna get it back lickety-split," I said. A wrestling match was going on in my belly.

He squinted at me like he was trying to see inside my head and decide for himself whether I was fibbing or not.

"First you go and leave your abuela's Bible at your friend's house, and now you lose track of the amulet. It's the closest thing you've got to connect you to her past. By hook or crook, you find it, you hear?"

"Yes sir," I said. "I'll get it right back. I know where it is." It was a white lie, but I couldn't stand Pappy thinking I'd lost it for real.

That night, I lay in bed, trying to picture every possible place I coulda left or dropped the amulet. I decided that the next morning, I'd leave a little early for school so's I could search the ground on the way there and check all around the outside of the schoolhouse. My aching nose wouldn't let me fall asleep and kept me up replaying the fight with Virgil.

I flashed on when I'd been on the ground with Virgil on top of me. I got a sudden sick feeling that the amulet had dropped outta my pocket then. I don't even think I slept a wink all night, tossing and turning with worry that Virgil had gotten his grubby hands on it. What if the last person on earth I'd ever want seeing or knowing anything about my amulet had picked it up and was holding on to it? I felt like I musta been having a nightmare, except that I was wide awake.

Chapter 22
Finders Keepers, Losers Weepers

"Lose somethin', lightnin' boy?" Virgil said the next morning when he saw me looking around my desk. He was waving my amulet with his grimy fingers!

"Gimme that! It's mine!" I yelled and reached over to snatch it from him, but he held it up higher. He was about a foot taller than me. I wished Paul woulda hurried up and gotten to school already so he coulda grabbed it for me.

"Ever hear of finders keepers? What is this ugly old thing anyway? You dig it up outta the dirt somewhere?" Virgil said.

Now, I coulda suffered Virgil's mouth as much as I had to, but this time he'd gone too far. I rammed my head into his stomach like a bull charging a red flag. But knocking him down didn't make him let go of the amulet. Then the outside school bell clanged, and Miss Pritchert came into the classroom in time to see Virgil struggling to get up, with me pinning him down.

"James! That's enough!" she hollered. It didn't look too good for me. "Class, take your seats. And you, James, go sit over there in the corner." She got the dunce cap and set it on my head.

I sorely wanted to tell Miss Pritchert that I was just trying to get something back that Virgil had stolen from me, but she woulda wanted to know what it was. I couldn't let anybody else find out about the amulet, so I kept quiet.

"You'll be staying in for recess, and you'll be seeing me after school as well," Miss Pritchert said, shaking her head at me.

"Best learn how to stop pickin' fights, you little pip-squeak. Otherwise, you might end up in the same place as your mama." Virgil laughed.

I spent the whole school day in the corner with that dopey dunce cap on my head. It was the longest day of my life. The worst part of it was that Fanny had to see me like that. I woulda preferred having my knuckles rapped with a ruler. After Miss

Pritchert rang the bell at the end of the day, I had to face her.

"Didn't I just speak to you yesterday about controlling your temper, James? It's surprising to me that as bright a boy as you are, you forget to think before you act. If this happens again, I'll have no choice but to expel you from school. And I'm quite certain your pappy will not be too pleased." Even the stray hairs that had escaped from her bun looked angry.

Miss Pritchert had me write one hundred times, "I will never fight at school." On top of that, I had to clean all the desks, sweep the floor, and bang the erasers outside. That chalk dust threw me into a coughing spell.

Scrubbing all those desks with a wet rag gave a fella time to gather up his courage to get something back that belonged to him.

***

The next day, on the way to school, I met up with Paul.

"What is it you fight with Virgil about yesterday?" he asked.

"Remember the charm from my abuela that I showed you? Well, Virgil stole it. I got plans to go gettin' it back, and I sure could use some help."

"I am ready to help you," Paul said, nodding. "What plan you have?"

"Tell you later," I said just as Miss Pritchert rang the bell and we had to go into the schoolhouse.

At lunch recess, Paul and I charged outside with the rest of the kids like a stampede of buffalo. But we didn't stand around waiting to be picked by the team captains for Wolf over the River. Paul and me were always the last ones picked anyway.

Instead, while the others were all deciding on their teams, we snuck back into the classroom. Luckily, it was empty 'cause Miss Pritchert had gone on one of her lunchtime walks.

We searched inside Virgil's battered desk, but all's we found was a wad of chewing gum, a pencil with a broken point, a shooter marble he probably stole from someone, and a tattered copy of *The Boxcar Children*. Who woulda guessed that Virgil liked the same books that I did? The thing was, though, I had read that book a long time ago, back when I was in third grade. We didn't find what we were looking for, so we closed Virgil's desk and crept back outside.

By then, the two teams were lined up on opposite sides of the dirt playing field, getting ready to start. Margaret was the wolf who got to stand in the "river"—the middle of the field. Paul and I stood on the side like a coupla useless rocks, hoping we could still get into the game.

"Come on, James, be on our team!" Fanny called. My heart felt like it was gonna pop straight outta my chest.

Paul threw me one of his half grins and gave me a little shove toward the field.

"Hey, Russia boy, over here!" Fiona called out, waving Paul over to the other team.

To start the game, Margaret yelled, "Wolf over the river! Don't lend a hand! Wolf over the river! Catch all you can!"

I charged down the field trying to get to safety across the make-believe river. I was scrawny, but that didn't mean I wasn't fast. I glanced over my shoulder and saw Fanny, her yellow curls bouncing as she ran. Margaret, the wolf, was gaining on her, about to tag her. I ran back a few steps, grabbed Fanny's hand, and pulled her along with me. After we made it safely across the river, we stopped running and bent over to catch our breath.

"Thanks," she said in between gulps of air. We both looked down at our hands, which were still attached, and let go as quick as a hiccup. She didn't even bother wiping her hand on her dress, though. That musta meant she didn't think I had cooties.

The school bell clanged. On our way back into the schoolhouse, Fanny looked me square in the eyes, smiled, and said, "You're the fastest runner I ever did see."

I walked around the rest of the day feeling so tall I coulda touched the clouds. I was even ready to take on Virgil.

Since we hadn't found the amulet in his desk, Paul and I agreed to pay ourselves a little visit to Virgil's house after school. Expecting that it might take some doing to locate the amulet, I had told Pappy another itty-bitty white lie that morning. I'd said I might be late to the diner after school on account of I'd be busy working on a school project with Paul. Well, depending on how you looked at it, this was a sorta project—the getting-back-a-piece-of-my-history project.

We needed to catch Virgil by himself, away from his posse. Since they usually all walked home together, we waited awhile before leaving school to make sure he'd be alone at his house by the time we got there. I didn't really have much of a plan other than thinking that two boys confronting Virgil would be better than one. Especially when one of the two was a lot bigger and stronger than Virgil.

And whatever my plan was, it depended on Virgil's daddy not being around. I sure wasn't keen on us running into him, remembering the things my mama had told me about him, especially about him having a real mean temper. Lately, Virgil had been telling everybody that his daddy was working on the oil rig, so I was praying that's where he'd be today. If only Virgil's mama was still around, I was sure she woulda made him give me back what belonged to me. But she up and ran off to California with a city man who was passing through. Mama had said it was the smartest thing Virgil's mama ever did.

Virgil's house was as mangy as he was. One of the front porch posts was so bent that it looked like an old man hunched over. There were enough empty bootleg bottles, corncobs, and bullet shells scattered on the ground that the place coulda been mistook for a junkyard. It was like there was a garden of trash growing in place of beans and tomatoes.

We snuck up to the front door. I didn't know about Paul, but I was as nervous as a fly in a glue pot. I sure wasn't feeling tall enough to touch the clouds anymore. Paul knocked on the air and gave me a questioning look. I nodded and knocked real lightly. Nobody came to the door, so I put my ear to it. Not hearing any life coming from inside, I hoped that meant Virgil's daddy was off working and Virgil was home by himself, probably sitting in there thinking up more rotten things he could do to me and Paul. We both knocked harder.

"Who's out there?!" roared a voice from inside—a voice that sounded a whole lot older and scarier than Virgil's. Paul and I took a few steps back. Suddenly, the door burst open like a tornado had yanked it off its hinges. Virgil's daddy stood in the doorway. His hair was black and stringy, and his face was as red and puffy as a prizefighter's. Paul and I were pasted to the front porch, too scared to move.

Virgil's daddy raised the bottle he was holding and shook it at us. "You varmints, get off my property!"

He stumbled toward us, and somehow, we got our feet unstuck and jumped off that porch. We sped away like we were escaping a burning house. When we looked over our shoulders, we saw Virgil's daddy weaving down the road after us, hollering and shaking his bottle. That was the second time that day that me being a fast runner came in handy.

As soon as we got close to the diner, we looked back again, and Virgil's daddy was nowhere in sight. He mighta been too drunk to keep chasing us, but we weren't about to stop running to find out. Like Pappy was fond of saying, a dead snake can still bite.

"No wonder Virgil's meaner than a mama wasp," I said, in between breaths, once we stopped. "He takes after his daddy."

Paul was bent over, breathing hard. "This did not work, James. We must find some other way to get from Virgil your charm."

"You got any bright ideas how to make that shmendrick give it back?" I didn't know if I'd said the word right, but Paul lifted a corner of his mouth like he did when he thought something was funny.

"How about we hike to crater on Sunday and make a different plan, okay?" he said.

"Yeah, let's do that. Thanks for coming to Virgil's with me. See ya tomorrow, Paul."

He took off, and I stayed outside the diner for a while, catching my breath and wiping the sweat off my brow. Otherwise, Pappy woulda wanted to know why working on a school project had left me looking like I'd been trying to outrun the great Jim Thorpe.

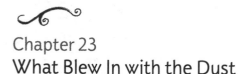

Chapter 23
What Blew In with the Dust

The next day, I aimed to get myself back on Miss Pritchert's good side and stay clear of Virgil's fists. We had an arithmetic test, and I scored higher than anybody else, except Paul, who was just as good at numbers as I was. And he shoulda done better than me anyhow on account of he was older. Fanny told me she thought I was real smart for doing so well on the test. She made me feel like all my troubles had run away. I tried to say thanks, but my voice got stuck in my throat. All in all, it was a pretty fine day. But my good feelings soured soon as I reached into my pocket to rub my amulet, forgetting for two seconds that it was gone, and found nothing but a few grains of sand.

That night, I dreamt there was a screeching hawk circling above me. It was carrying something small and coin-like in its talons. It mighta been my amulet. When I stretched my arms way up to the sky to reach for the hawk, they turned into wings. I flapped them till I flew up to meet the hawk, and together we soared over the town. While we were flying, the hawk dropped the thing it was holding. From high up in the sky, I saw miniature versions of Mama and Pappy and Paul and Virgil below me. I saw everybody I knew except Abuela. In the dream, I heard her voice say, "I'm right here," and felt the hawk's wings flapping next to me. Then I woke up.

It was finally Friday, usually my favorite day of the week 'cause it meant a whole weekend was stretched out before me. But when I got outta bed, I couldn't concentrate on anything except how badly I wanted to get my amulet back, and I was sore at myself for not figuring out some way to get Virgil to cough it up. That morning, the sky was fulla angry clouds to match my mood.

At school, Virgil was quieter than usual. No name-calling and no mean comments shot from his mouth. I was worried, though, 'cause maybe that meant he had some anger building up and was looking for just the right excuse to let it explode—most likely all over me. I wasn't gonna wait around to find out what kinda mood he was in, so the minute the bell rang, I hightailed it to the diner.

The sky looked even angrier than before. There was a bank of dirty-brown clouds gathering off in the distance, and the wind started picking up. I took off running. I wasn't gonna wait till those clouds caught up with me. They had the makings of one of those dust devils we'd get sometimes on real hot summer days—but we never expected them to come in the fall.

Then the clouds started spitting sand—sand that was rough and scratchy and made my eyes smart. I pulled my bandanna outta a pocket of my over-alls and covered my nose and mouth with it. It was thanks to Abuela that I had that bandanna with me. Me being caught in one of these Texas sandstorms was exactly what she had in mind when she gave it to me and told me to carry it with me all the time. I wished I had something to protect my eyes too.

I kept trying to run, but it took me forever to get to Ridgely's on account of I was fighting against the wind, and the wind was winning. The sky was murky and thick with sand, making it hard to see the path right in front of me. I broke out in a sweat, afraid I wasn't gonna make it to the diner before it was impossible to find my way. The wind howled like a coyote, and I was afraid nobody would hear me if I called for help.

Finally, I could make out the diner just a few yards away. I sucked in a big breath of relief, which made me cough. Getting inside was a challenge. I had to play a game of tug-of-war with the front door. Every time I yanked it open, the wind slammed it shut. Then Pappy came to the door and forced it open long enough to pull me inside.

"I'm mighty glad to see you, Butch," he said, putting his arm around me and giving my shoulder a squeeze. "Sure wasn't expectin' a storm like this. Seems like two minutes ago there was nothin'. Then all of a sudden, the wind starts roarin' and that blanket of sand covers the sky. Just the other day, Malvern was jokin' about how in one of these sandstorms you can catch sight of the towns of Lubbock and Amarillo blowin' by."

Pappy took me into the kitchen and went over to the sink. He wet down a towel and handed it to me. "Here, Butch, dab your eyes, but don't rub. You don't want the sand to scratch 'em up."

The cool damp cloth was soothing. "This sandstorm sure is a doozy," I said. "Never saw one this big. When do ya figure it'll stop?"

"There was a fierce one some years back—before you were born, I reckon—that lasted four or five days. That time, the sand particles rose higher than a utility pole. There's no telling how long this'll go on. If we're lucky, it'll just roll through."

The diner was emptier than the streets of Odessa at 9 p.m. "We best be closin' up," said Pappy. "Nobody in their right mind's gonna come out in this storm for a bite to eat."

He wrapped up the meat, stuck it in the giant icebox, and put the onions and potatoes back in the bins. Before leaving, we shoved wet rags under the door to keep the sand out and covered our faces with damp bandannas. It was a good thing we lived next door 'cause otherwise we woulda had to wait out the storm at the diner, and there was no way of knowing how long we woulda been stuck in there.

Just since I'd fought my way home from school, the storm had gotten worse. It was one giant dragon, but instead of breathing fire, it was blowing sand and dust on everything in its path. As soon as we stepped outside, I saw tumbleweeds whipping by.

Pappy kept a firm grip on my arm, and together we pushed against the wind, trying to walk the ten yards to the house. We were facing a wall of sand.

I put my arm up to shield my eyes. You wouldn't know it was only late afternoon 'cause the storm had turned the sky so dark we could hardly see across the road. The gusts of sand felt like a thousand needles pricking my bare hands.

Suddenly, Pappy pulled me in the opposite direction—away from our house and toward Elbert Heath's field instead. "Can you see that?" Pappy shouted over the roar of the storm. He pointed ahead of us at the ground.

Something was lying in a big heap in the dirt. It looked an awful lot like a sack of potatoes that had fallen off a truck. All's I wanted to do was get inside, away from the blowing sand that was stinging my eyes something fierce. But Pappy yelled, "Stay near me!" and dragged me toward the pile on the ground. We could hear faint moaning. I figured it was a dog that musta lost its way and got knocked down in the storm.

"It's a kid!" Pappy hollered as we got closer.

Crouching down, we saw that the boy was half buried in the sand. His eyes were clamped shut, and he was curled up like a hibernating groundhog, not moving a muscle. If it wasn't for the little whimpering sounds coming from his mouth, I woulda feared he had gone to join the worms.

"Help me get him up!" Pappy yelled.

We each grabbed ahold of an arm and heaved him up. He was too big for Pappy to carry, so we draped his arms over our shoulders. Shoving against the wind with all our might, we dragged him to the house. I tugged hard to yank the front door open, and once we got him inside, the wind blew the door shut. The house was dark, and the air was thick from the dust that had blown in.

"What in tarnation were you doin' wanderin' around out there in a sandstorm like this, boy?" Pappy asked.

He answered with nothing but moans and groans. We laid him out on my bed and wiped the sand and dust off his face with a wet washrag. He started coughing and spitting up sand.

"Good thing we came along. He was suffocatin' out there," Pappy said to me. "You know this boy?"

"Yeah," I said. "This here's Virgil." What I wanted to say was that this dust lump lying in my bed was the last person on earth I'd want to rescue from anything.

"Leroy Jackson's boy? The one who's been givin' you all the trouble?"

I nodded and put my shushing finger to my

mouth, not wanting Pappy to say anything more about Virgil in front of him. All I needed was for Virgil to think I was going home after school and crying a river of tears to Pappy about him. It'd give him one more reason to come after me.

"I sure wish Marlena were here. She'd know exactly what to do for this boy," Pappy said. I couldn't tell if Pappy's eyes were red and watery from the dust or 'cause he was missing Abuela.

Virgil exploded into another coughing fit. It seemed like it went on forever, like he was coughing up his whole insides.

"I can try to help him," I said. "I remember pretty good some healin' things I learned from Abuela. All that coughin' is his body's way of tryin' to get rid of the dust and sand that's cloggin' up his lungs. Abuela woulda said he's got mal aire. And I think I know the remedies for that."

Pappy and I were doing our share of coughing too, but we hadn't swallowed nearly as much dust as Virgil had. He musta been out there in the storm for a spell. I thought even Virgil woulda had enough sense to not be out wandering in this mess.

Before I got to tending to Virgil, I wetted down a clean cloth to wipe the dust and sand from my own eyes. I handed another one to Pappy, and he cleaned his eyes too. Then I went into the kitchen and searched through Abuela's jars of herbs and tea leaves till I found what I was looking for.

I mixed up some chaparral, mullein, butterfly weed, sage, and peppermint with boiling water and let it steep for a while. After we wiped Virgil's eyes as clean as we could get them, he finally opened them and commenced staring at me and Pappy like we each had three heads or something. We propped him up in my bed with some extra pillows. Virgil tried to speak, but he couldn't get much out without breaking into another coughing spell.

"Y-y-y-you, y-you . . ." he stuttered and pointed at me.

I imagined he was fixing to accuse me of causing the storm in the first place. Seeing as how he believed my family was cursed and all, I wouldn't have put anything past him.

"Drink this real slow-like," I said, offering Virgil the mug filled with the concoction I'd brewed. "And careful—it's pipin' hot."

"It's . . . i-i-it's . . . p-p-p-poison," he croaked, shaking his head.

"Come on, Virgil. It ain't gonna hurt you," I said.

"This tea'll help you breathe. You more'n likely got a bad case of dust pneumonia."

"It'll help you, son," Pappy said. Only after Pappy handed the mug to him did Virgil take a sip.

"Uck!" he cried and spit it out right on my bedsheets.

Pappy ordered him to drink the tea, telling him he wasn't gonna get any better if he didn't. So he drank it, making faces like he was fixing to puke with every gulp.

Meanwhile, my eyes got real heavy. Wrestling with the storm had sapped all the energy outta me. All I wanted to do was climb into my bed, but I couldn't on account of it was occupied by my least favorite person on earth. Virgil had already shut his eyes and dozed off.

"Why don't you go take a nap on the sofa, Butch?" Pappy suggested. "I'm afraid you're gonna have to sleep there for a bit till we get this boy in better shape."

I went out to the living room. Before I stretched out on the sofa, I brushed off a layer of storm dust that had settled on it. I had to rest my head on one of Abuela's fancy embroidered pillows, and it was scratchy on my cheek.

Pappy rolled up wet towels and packed them around our windows and hung sheets over them, trying to keep any more sand from getting in. The storm was still making a racket outside when I fell asleep.

I don't rightly know how long I slept, but when I woke up it was real quiet outside. The white sheet Pappy had put up over the window had turned brown. I got up and lifted it to take a peek outside, but the glass was too covered with dust for me to see anything. I heard Pappy in my room talking to Virgil, who was coughing and coughing. Virgil's eyes were still closed when I went in there.

"Did the storm pass, Pappy?" I asked him.

"I believe so," he said.

"How long did I sleep, anyhow?" I asked, looking at Virgil taking over my bed.

"You slept all the way till this morning. But your friend here had a rough night. He was literally coughin' up a storm."

Virgil blinked his eyes open. "Where can we find your daddy?" Pappy asked him. "We need to let him know that you're okay and bring him over to see you."

"P-p-please . . ." Virgil said, before breaking out in a coughing fit. "D-d-don't tell him where I am, sir."

"Why not, son?" Pappy asked in the kinda comforting voice he'd used with me when I was so sad after Abuela passed.

It was the first time I ever saw Virgil looking downright scared. Suddenly, he started bawling. "I . . . I . . . don't know what my pa is gonna do to me," Virgil managed to get out in between his crying and coughing.

I never thought I'd say this, but I felt downright sorry for him. Taking pity on Virgil was a feeling so different for me that it was akin to putting on a stiff new pair of overalls before they got worn in.

Pappy tried to calm him down. "It's okay. We'll talk about this later," he said, lightly patting Virgil's hand. "You rest now."

Pappy signaled me to follow him outta my room. "I gotta head on over to the diner, open up, and see what condition it's in after the storm," he said. "You keep an eye on him and give him some more of that tea—or do whatever else you think will help him mend."

The only thing good about having Virgil stay with us was that it got me outta working that Saturday. But I sure coulda thought of better ways to spend my time than looking after my worst enemy.

It turned out I didn't have to pay Virgil much heed on account of he slept mosta the day, in between coughing fits. It gave me a chance to start reading *White Fang* for my next school book report.

While Virgil was snoozing, I checked outside to see what things looked like after the storm. I found a thick blanket of sand all over the front porch, so I fetched the broom to sweep it off. I had trouble even recognizing what was around me. I could hardly make out the picket fence in front of our house on account of it was nearly buried under a pile of sand. I looked over at Elbert Heath's field, where we'd found Virgil. Elbert's plow was buried in so much sand that I could only see the top of it poking out.

Pappy came home after closing up the diner and asked me how Virgil was doing. I told him he'd spent the day sleeping and coughing.

"I'm fixin' to pay a visit to his daddy now, so can you keep lookin' after him for a bit?"

"But, Pappy, Virgil doesn't want his daddy to know where he is," I reminded him.

"Well, even a scoundrel like Leroy Jackson has a right to know what happened to his kid."

I told Pappy where to find the Jacksons' house, but he already knew where they lived.

"Trust me, it'll be okay," Pappy said. "I'll be back right soon."

When Virgil woke up, I made him drink another cup of Abuela's healing tea. At least this time, he actually took it from me and didn't spit it up. But he didn't hold back on making terrible faces while he drank it. And he didn't say thanks neither. Lucky for me, he dozed off right after, so I didn't have to talk to him. I woulda bet anything that if the tables were turned, Virgil woulda left me out in the storm to get buried alive.

I pulled a chair into my room and sat in the corner. Watching Virgil sleep, I got to wondering if he even had one nice bone in his body. I remembered Abuela telling me that everybody has some good inside of them, but in some people it's just buried a little deeper than in others. Even if I was having trouble finding that good part of Virgil, it didn't feel half bad helping him anyway.

I picked up my book and read while Virgil snored and coughed. By the time Pappy got back, it was dark as a pocket outside. When he came into my room, Virgil woke up.

"You shouldn't have a lick of trouble from your daddy going forward," Pappy told him.

"Y-y-you saw him?" Virgil's eyes got real wide, and he looked like he was gonna turn on the water-works again. His right eye started twitching.

"Don't you worry none, son—your daddy's gonna dry out and start behavin' like a father should. Or he's gonna have ole Jeb Ridgely to answer to." Pappy laid his big hand on Virgil's arm, trying to calm him down.

"W-w-what did my daddy say?" Virgil's voice was still shaking. "Is he comin' here to get me?"

"No, you're gonna stay with us till you're back on your feet," Pappy said. "When it's time, I'll take you home."

That scared puppy look faded from Virgil's face, and his eye quit twitching. He took a real full breath of relief, which set him off coughing again. I tried giving him a different kinda tea for the mal aire, one I made from a mix of elephant garlic and brown sugar. Then I rifled through Abuela's herb jars, looking for valerian root so's I could brew up another tea that I'd seen Abuela make for people who had trouble sleeping. And it worked 'cause Virgil slept right through the night, barely coughing at all. Or at least that's what Pappy told me the next morning, since I slept through the night too.

It was Sunday, so Pappy and I told Virgil we were going to church. Pappy said to him, "Don't go gettin' into any mischief while we're gone, you hear?" That was Pappy's idea of a joke on account of it was unlikely in Virgil's weak state that he was even gonna leave my bed, except to use the privy. I woulda bet my right arm that he was just gonna keep sleeping all day.

I was even more anxious than usual for church to be over with. I was itching to tell Paul why I couldn't hike to the crater with him.

"Quit your fidgetin', James," Pappy whispered. "You got ants in your pants?" I smiled, thinking, *At least I don't have twig girdlers in 'em.*

After the service, I didn't even wait around to say howdy to Fanny. I ran straight over to Paul's and shared my news. He thought I was telling a tall tale.

"Is not possible! How do you say . . . you pull my leg, yes?"

"I'm not pulling your leg or anythin' else! We got Virgil Jackson at my house, and if that ain't a fact, God's a possum," I told him. "And I'm not keen on havin' him there, waitin' on him hand and foot while he hogs my bed. But he's in a pretty bad way, so Pappy says we gotta take care of him till he gets well."

I made Paul swear not to tell the kids at school. We sealed it by spitting on our hands and doing our secret handshake. For the first time in a long time, I wasn't dreading going to school the next day, since I knew who wouldn't be there to bother me.

Chapter 24
Did My Purpose Find Me?

Splat! That's pretty much the sound my body made when I rolled off the sofa and landed smack-dab on the hardwood floor. It was Monday morning, and Virgil was still occupying my bed. I wished I could speed up his healing so he could go home and I could get my bed back. But I didn't know what else to do for him aside from giving him the special teas and feeding him hot soups.

I wasn't about to stay home from school just to keep a watch on him, and 'course Pappy had to work at the diner. The longest we'd left him alone was when we were at church, so I didn't cotton to the notion of letting him stay in our house on his own all day. Even though he was pretty weak and sleeping most of the time, he was still Virgil, and I didn't trust him as far as I could throw him.

After school, I headed straight home to check on Virgil instead of going to the diner to work. I found him right where I'd left him that morning—asleep with his head propped up on two pillows in my bed. I decided I'd suggest to Pappy that Virgil could rest up just as good on the sofa.

The whole time Virgil was at our house, I was bursting to tell him to hand over my amulet. I figured he owed me that much, seeing as how me and Pappy had saved his life. But I held my peace until I was certain he was feeling much better.

By the fourth day after the storm, Virgil finally got himself up and outta my bed for longer than just to use the privy. He started eating solid food too. He was coughing much less, and there was no more rattling in his throat.

Even taking care of someone as mean as Virgil gave me a good feeling, like when I got all the answers right on my arithmetic tests. Seeing how much he was improving got me to thinking that maybe that *was* my purpose. Even Pappy, who was real stingy when it came to heaping praise, said to me, "Butch, you're doin' a fine job helpin' Virgil. You've really got a knack for healin'. Maybe you oughta become a doctor."

Malvern had said that too. And I remembered Mama telling me that my daddy coulda been a doctor.

As the week wore on, the kids at school were making up all kinds of stories about why Virgil had been absent for so long. Chester claimed Virgil had wandered over to the deserted house by the creek to steal onions from the garden, like we all did from time to time. Everybody knew that house was haunted.

"But when Virgil crawled under the fence to pull out them onions, the ghost caught him red-handed, scared him to death, and dumped his body in the creek," Chester said.

Margaret had her own far-fetched theory. She told everyone that Virgil had gone to the oil rig with his daddy but got too close to the explosives they used at the wells.

"Virgil got blown to smithereens," Margaret said, putting on a sad face. "They found pieces of him all over the road."

Fanny, who had more sense than the rest of them put together, said, "I fear that Virgil got buried alive in the sandstorm, seein' as how the last time any of us laid eyes on him was here at school before the storm got goin'. I think we should all pray that he gets found."

I was sorely tempted to tell Fanny the truth and put her outta her worrying, but I couldn't. Paul and I had spit and shook hands on keeping it secret, and there was no breaking that. Besides, it felt satisfying, us being the only ones who knew the real story and laughing to ourselves at the other kids for making up their tall tales.

I decided that when I got home from school, I'd finally demand Virgil give me back my amulet. He wasn't feeling so poorly anymore. With the way he was behaving while he was recuperating at our house, you'd'a hardly known this was the same Virgil Jackson. He said "please" and "thank you" and "yes sir" when he was talking to Pappy, and he didn't go calling me any names. And even though he was still pretty weak, he took his dishes to the sink and washed them himself. I'd never seen him being so respectful before. Maybe the sandstorm had blown some of the meanness right outta him.

When I walked in the door, I found him sitting on the sofa—my new sleeping place—holding my book. I wasn't too happy about it, but I decided to shove that feeling aside. I figured that so long as

Virgil was in my house, I might as well make the best of it and try to find something good about him.

"You like Jack London?" I asked him.

"I never read nothin' by him," Virgil said. "This any good?"

"It's a real good read. You can borrow it when I'm done."

"Probably don't want to. Got a lotta big words in there," he said. I remembered what I'd seen in his school desk—the Boxcar book—and guessed he wasn't too good at reading.

"Your grandfather left a coupla slices of pie for us," Virgil said. "I waited for you before eatin'."

The two of us went over to the dining table and dug into the pie. It was pumpkin, one of my favorites.

"Your grandfather sure makes a mean pie," Virgil mumbled with his mouth full. "And he's real good to you too. You're lucky."

I just nodded. While we were snacking on the sweet, creamy pie, I started relating the stories the kids at school had been making up to explain Virgil's absence. Soon as I told him about the ghost at the haunted house that supposedly scared the bejeezus outta him, he laughed and coughed so hard he spit up pumpkin. Flecks of orange goop hung off the tip of his nose, and some even flew over and landed on my arm. With Virgil's spirits being so high, it seemed like the right time to ask.

"Hey Virgil, where's my charm? I need it back."

He swiped the pumpkin off his face with the back of his hand. "I ain't got any idea what you're talkin' about," he said, looking down at the table.

"Come on, Virgil. You know what I mean. Remember that little round metal thing you were wavin' in front of me and sayin', *Finders keepers?*"

He kept his eyes glued to his empty pie plate.

"Oh yeah, uh . . . now I remember. Don't rightly know what happened to it. It didn't look like nothin' special." A bout of coughing overtook him.

"It was somethin' special," I said, my anger rising. "Real special. Come on, Virgil—what'd you do with it?"

"I don't know where it is, I swear," he said in between coughs.

My right hand closed up into a tight fist. If Virgil hadn't looked so sickly, I woulda broken Pappy's rule right there and then. To keep my fist from doing what it had a hankering to do, I stormed outta the room. I grabbed my book and took it out to the front porch. I sat out there trying to get lost in the Yukon

Territory with *White Fang*. The end of Virgil's stay with us wasn't gonna come soon enough for me.

When Pappy came home, he took one look at me on the porch and said, "Whatya got your tail up about, Butch?"

"I'm fine, Pappy," I snapped. I didn't want to let on to him what was eating at me. I wasn't about to fess up that I'd dropped the amulet while I was fighting with Virgil. Pappy might never forgive me. And lucky for me, Pappy musta had more important things on his mind, 'cause he hadn't even brought up the missing amulet since I'd told him I misplaced it.

Pappy said Virgil was finally well enough to get on home. Boy, was I thankful for that.

"Are you finally ready to tell me what you were doin' wanderin' around in a sandstorm?" Pappy asked Virgil.

"I had to get away from my daddy 'fore he killed me," Virgil said. "He gets awfully mean when he's drinkin'. I ran outside and saw the sandstorm brewin' but decided to take my chances. Figured the sandstorm wouldn't hurt nearly as bad as whatever my daddy might do to me."

Hearing that got me feeling sorry for him again. I couldn't help thinking about how often I wished

235

I still had a daddy. But maybe I was better off than Virgil. I wouldn't have wanted to have a daddy like his. Sure, my daddy was struck down by lightning, but like Mama had said, Virgil musta been afraid of lightning striking at his house all the time.

Chapter 25
Maybe a Tiger Can Change His Stripes
(a Little)

The next day, when Pappy drove Virgil back to
his house, he stayed inside for a while to make sure
Virgil's daddy wasn't gonna give Virgil any trouble.
I didn't rightly know what Pappy had said to Leroy
Jackson, but I knew what people said about my pappy.
I remembered one time asking Malvern to help
me with my homework assignment—making up
sentences with our vocabulary words. *Persuasive* was
one of the words on the list, and Malvern had said,
"Jeb Ridgely has no trouble convincin' people to see
things his way, because he can be awfully *persuasive*."

When Virgil came swaggering back to school,
the other kids treated him like he was Charles
Lindbergh returning from his solo flight across the

Atlantic. They surrounded him and asked where he'd been over the past few days. I could hardly believe my ears when I heard him bragging about how he went out in the sandstorm to save Widow Carson's cat and how he caught dust pneumonia while he was being the big hero. Paul and I looked at each other and rolled our eyes.

Soon as Virgil saw me, he switched to his tough voice. "Hey lightnin' boy. Got somethin' to say to you after school."

I got to thinking that maybe I'd made one gigantic mistake by saving his hide. I wondered if Pappy and I shoulda just left him out in the dust storm to suffocate. But then I figured that if I was truly gonna be a healer or a doctor someday, I might get stuck having to help scoundrels like Virgil from time to time. I guess I couldn't pick who got sick. If somebody needed my help, I was gonna help them.

I had trouble concentrating on my lessons all day, fretting about what Virgil was gonna do to me after school. During recess, I asked Paul to stick by me after school.

"Of course I stay with you," he said. "But after you rescued Virgil from the storm, I think he not bother you anymore."

"Yeah, that's what I thought too. Guess a tiger don't change its stripes. That's what my mama says."

"How can tigers change stripes?"

"Never mind," I said. I didn't feel like explaining the expression just then.

After school, Paul and I found Virgil waiting for me on the path home. He squeezed his right hand into a fist. I was sure as a kettle's black that he was meaning to use that fist to clobber me with. My belly was knotting up.

He raised his chin and nodded at Paul, saying, "He don't need to be here."

"He's stayin'," I said, trying to keep my voice from sounding too shaky.

Then Virgil raised up his closed hand and opened it, palm up.

The amulet! He had it! My belly finally unknotted, and the rest of me sorta loosened up. It was like I'd been clenching ahold of something inside for a long time, and I was finally letting it go.

"Just wanted to give this back to you," he said, handing it to me. "And to . . . to . . . um . . . thank you for what you did for me . . . healin' me and all."

"Sure," I said, taking the amulet from his hand and slipping it into my pocket. I was relieved that I wasn't gonna have to practice my blocking moves. Clearly Virgil wasn't fixing to wallop me. "I thought you said you didn't know what happened to it," I reminded him.

"I just said that 'cause . . . 'cause I didn't know if it was gonna still be where I left it. What is it, anyhow, and what's that writin' on there say?"

"I can't read what it says, but I know it's called an amulet. My grandmother gave it to me 'fore she died, and that's why it's so important to me," I said. "So thanks for returnin' it."

"Yeah, okay. It don't mean we're friends or nothin', mind you." As he walked off he added, "Well, see ya 'round . . . James." He nodded in Paul's direction. "And you . . ."

Paul stood, shaking his head. "That is not Virgil. This is the first time he not call me a bad name. You cure him of more than dust sickness, James."

"Maybe so," I said. I crossed my fingers behind my back that Virgil wasn't gonna go back to his old ways—taunting us and picking fights with me.

"Hey, thanks for stickin' by me," I said to Paul. "Let's keep what just happened with Virgil to ourselves. Shake on it?" I spit on my hand and held it out. Paul spit on his, and we did our secret handshake.

***

I rushed to Ridgely's. Pappy was in the kitchen, chopping up onions.

"Look what I found," I announced, holding up the amulet.

"I'm mighty glad you found it," Pappy said. Tears were streaming down his cheeks.

"You don't have to cry about it, Pappy," I teased him, knowing full well the onions were to blame.

Pappy actually chuckled, something that happened about as often as a meteor fell from the sky. Then he set down the knife and patted my head with the hand that wasn't all stunk up with onions.

"You're growin' up, James," he said, bending down and looking me straight in the eyes. "You proved that with the fine job you did curin' Virgil. Now you keep that amulet in a safe place this time, you hear?"

"Yes sir," I said and shoved it deep into my pocket. Since Pappy was happy with me just then, it seemed like a good time to ask him for something.

"Pappy, I need to see Mama. When can we visit her?" I knew we couldn't see her so much anymore since they'd moved her to that hospital far away, but

I missed her, and I had a lot on my mind I wanted to share with her.

"Well, in another two weeks I'll be closin' up the diner for Christmas," Pappy said. "How about we pay her a visit then?"

It was gonna be a long coupla weeks, but at least I was gonna get to see her.

Then Pappy added, "Let's hope she's doin' much better by then."

"If she is, can we bring her home with us?" I asked, reaching into my pocket to rub the amulet. It was comforting having it back with me again.

Pappy laid his hand on my shoulder. "I guess we'll just have to wait and see, Butch."

"That'd be the best Christmas present ever," I said, and I sure meant it.

Chapter 26
My Brand-New Holiday

"It's chilly as a frosted frog out there this morning, so you best bundle up," Pappy said when I was getting dressed for school. It was about a week after I'd gotten the amulet back from Virgil. "And come straight home this afternoon to help me put up the Christmas decorations in the diner, you hear?" he told me.

On my way to school, I blew puffs of my breath into the air. I didn't mind the cold one bit after suffering through a summer and fall where the heat went on and on—even longer than Reverend Crawford's sermons. And the colder weather meant that Christmas was right around the corner.

I no longer dreaded going to school, worrying about what Virgil might do to me. As usual, whenever somebody from his posse was in earshot, Virgil snarled at me like a dog when another dog steals its bone. But if nobody else was around, he actually said howdy to me and didn't call me any names. He hadn't laid a hand on me since the sandstorm. He didn't bother Paul none either.

After the ending bell rang, I told Paul I had to go help Pappy with the Christmas decorations. He pursed his lips and squinched up his whole face like he did when he was in some kinda deep thought.

"Since you are Jewish too, that means you celebrate Chanukah, yes?" Paul asked. He said the name of the holiday like he had a fish bone stuck in the back of his throat.

"I don't think so. I never even heard of it till you told me about it."

"You will see. You come to my house tomorrow night when Chanukah begins. And come with much hunger."

"I think you mean I should bring my appetite, right?"

"Hmm, I think so," he said. "Bring that and your hunger too."

Pappy agreed to let me go over to Paul's the next night. "I don't know the first thing about their

244

holiday, but it's high time you learned somethin' about the religion of your abuela's ancestors," he said. "I know you already told your friend about your family history, but I still don't want you blabbin' it to anybody else, you hear?"

Since Pappy was so keen on me keeping this Jewish part of me hidden, I a-feared he wasn't gonna cotton to what I had in mind to do with my amulet. After I showed Pappy that I got it back, I took to keeping it in my bureau drawer, but I missed being able to have it with me during the day. So I threaded a string through the little loop on it. The next afternoon, when I was fixing to go over to Paul's for his holiday, I showed Pappy the amulet dangling on the string.

"Would it be okay if I wore it around my neck?" I asked. "That way I'll be sure to never lose it again. And I'll only wear it underneath my shirt, so nobody but me and you will know it's there."

"Hmm." Pappy stroked his beard and studied my face like he was reading a book. He took forever to answer. "I guess it's as good a place as any to keep it. But promise me that you'll make sure it's hidden real well under your shirt."

"I promise, Pappy," I said.

Before I headed over to Paul's house, Pappy gave me a plate of gingerbread Christmas cookies. "Take these with you. Just baked 'em," he said. "Don't want you to show up for their holiday celebration empty-handed."

It was still plenty light out while I was walking there. I heard that *kee-eeeee-ar* screeching sound coming from the sky and looked up to see a red hawk circling above me. I got to wondering if it was the same hawk from before, if it was Abuela's spirit guiding me again. I figured Abuela woulda been right happy that I was on my way to learn something about a holiday her ancestors celebrated.

***

As soon as Paul opened the door, I handed him the cookies. "Here, my pappy made these for you and said to wish you happy Christmas," I said.

Paul looked at me funny. "Thank you. I will give them to my muter. But we do not celebrate Christmas, so please do not wish her happy Christmas."

"Right," I said. I guessed I had a lot to learn.

When I walked in, Paul's whole family seemed a little bit—I dunno—friendlier, maybe? I asked

Paul if he'd told them about me having some Jewish ancestors.

"Of course I not tell them. I never tell what we say at the crater." Paul frowned. "That is our deal, yes?"

I believed him, but still . . . his family sure did seem to be acting different toward me. Paul's mama half smiled at me, which was 50 percent more than she'd ever done before. It was clear where Paul got his partial smile from. And when Paul gave her the cookies, she doubly surprised me by coming over and kissing me on the forehead. Paul's stepfather patted my head. Paul's bubby came out of the kitchen, her face glistening, and said, *"Zay gezunt"* as she pinched my cheeks. Her hands felt like they had cooking oil on them.

"What'd she say?" I asked Paul.

"She wishes you to be healthy," he said.

The smell of frying food floated through the house. My stomach must have sounded like an erupting volcano 'cause I'd brought my hunger and my appetite too, just like Paul had said. I was more than ready to taste whatever Paul's mama, his bubby, and his aunt Yetta were cooking up in the kitchen.

While Paul and I were waiting around for dinner, I went over to the bookcase in the living room.

I noticed that the printing on the spines of most of the books looked like the writing on my amulet. I was fixing to say something about it to Paul when Frieda came and grabbed my hand. She pulled me over to the dinner table where the family was gathering.

It was set all fancy like it had been that time I'd walked in on them during their Sabbath. Sitting smack-dab in the center of the table on top of a white lace tablecloth, looking mighty ancient, was that thing Paul called a menorah. It had eight little candleholders lined up in a neat row and another one in the middle that was perched up a little higher behind the others. The back plate was decorated with pictures of swords crossed over each other.

Uncle Ruvin poured a little oil in the first candleholder on one end of the menorah and some more in the holder that sat above the others. Aunt Yetta struck a match and lit the wicks. At the same time, everybody started chanting.

"These are Hebrew blessings we say on this holiday," Paul whispered to me.

When they stopped chanting, Frieda told me to sit in the seat in between her and Paul. "Wait'll you try Muter's latkes," she said. From Frieda's voice, you could hardly tell she wasn't from Texas. The dead giveaway was when she called her mama "muter" and 'course when she said "latkes," some food nobody from Texas woulda heard of. It turned out they were crispy brown potato fritters—the best I ever tasted.

Without even waiting for Paul's mama to say "Ess, ess," I got busy stuffing myself. Pappy always said that for a little guy, I sure knew how to eat. The latkes were mighty tasty but also awful greasy. I understood why after Paul explained how on Chanukah they were supposed to eat foods fried in a lotta oil.

"Long, long ago, the Jews were ruled by Syrian Greeks who did not let them follow Jewish ways," Paul said.

"Sounds like what happened to the Jewish people in Spain," I said.

Paul went on. "A small group of Jews, they fight against the rulers, and they win. But the Jews' temple was destroyed. When Jews went there to light candles, they find only oil enough for one day."

"But the oil lasted for eight whole days!" Frieda cried.

"*Sha*, Frieda," Paul said. "Let me finish telling the story." He gave Frieda a stern look. "It was miracle that the oil lasted so long. Is why we celebrate with lighting candles for eight nights and eating foods cooked in much oil."

After we finished eating, the grown-ups did something I never saw before. Truth was, everything I saw that night was new to me. They took teaspoons of sugar soaked with brandy, lit them on fire, and dunked them into glasses of tea. Paul called it a flaming tea ceremony. I didn't know how they got ahold of the brandy, Texas being a dry state and all. They sure had some different customs. This was one I couldn't wait to tell Mama about, but I figured I'd leave out the part with the brandy.

While the grown-ups were drinking their spiked tea, Frieda disappeared for a minute. She rushed back in waving a spinning top in her hand, her frizzy black hair poking outta her kerchief every which way.

"Pinkus, let's play dreidel!" she cried.

The three of us sat cross-legged on the floor. Frieda said the top was called a dreidel, and Paul explained the rules of the game. We each got ten peanuts as playing pieces and had to put one in the middle to start. I went first, getting a pretty good spin on the dreidel. There were different Hebrew letters on each side, and the letter the dreidel landed on when it stopped spinning told you how many peanuts you got to take or had to put in.

"You land on the letter *hay*," Paul said. "It means you take half of the pot."

"What's half of three peanuts?" Frieda asked.

"Is better if we have even number of players," Paul said. He called Ruvin over and asked him to play with us, probably 'cause his English was the best. Ruvin agreed, but he didn't sit on the floor. He crouched down whenever it was his turn to spin, his knees crackling like logs in a fire. By the time we finished playing, I'd won loads of peanuts on account of the dreidel kept landing on *gimmel*, which meant I got to take the whole pot.

"Do you like our holiday?" Frieda asked me.

"I like it fine. I like that in the end the Jews didn't get clobbered by the Greeks. And I sure am fond of your mama's potato latkes, and I like this dreidel spinnin' game too. I think I'm gonna like bein' a little Jewish." It slipped out before I could catch it. I tried to scoop it back up. "I mean, I'm not Jewish or anything. That's not what I meant," I said to Frieda. "I just meant that it seems like it . . . it wouldn't be so bad."

"The whole family knows you are. You don't

have to hide it from us," Frieda said. She squeezed my hand and flashed me a giant smile that showed off her missing front tooth. "You're kinda like part of our family now."

All of a sudden, a warm feeling flooded my insides, like the feeling I used to get when Abuela hugged me or when Mama listened hard to me or when Fanny smiled at me. Maybe I finally had what Abuela called *un corazón lleno*—a full heart. But I wondered just how Paul's family already knew about the Jewish in me. I didn't think I looked any different.

I looked at Paul for some answers. "You said you didn't say anything."

"Is true," he said. "Since you showed my family the metal piece with the picture of the menorah and the Hebrew writing—and then the Bible with more Hebrew writing—they believe you are Jewish."

I guess I shouldn'ta been too surprised at that. Why else would I have those things? I was a little worried, though, about Pappy being angry with me for letting my secret get out. But I figured he wouldn't mind so much that Paul's family knew. After all, Pappy said he wanted me to learn some-thing about the Jewish faith. And he sure wouldn't have to worry about Paul's family treating me poorly on account of me being part Jewish.

I started piecing together some stuff in my head like I was working on a puzzle—the amulet from Abuela, seeing the hawk at the crater and it showing up again in my dream and soaring over me on my way to Paul's, and then being with his family for their holiday. I got to thinking that maybe they were all signs leading me to discover my purpose—some purpose besides me helping people get well. Maybe I was supposed to learn what I could about the part of Abuela and me that was Jewish. I pressed my hand against my chest to feel the amulet under my shirt. Could a fella have more than one purpose? That was something I was gonna try to remember to ask Pappy and Mama about.

It was getting late, so I started saying my goodbyes.

"Thank you kindly, ma'am, for all the good food," I said to Paul's mama, rubbing my belly to help her understand what I was saying.

"You velcome here anytime, James," she said. "Zay gezunt." Then she came right up and hugged me.

After she let go, Samuel patted me on the head and Ruvin said, "Come back soon, boychik."

I left Paul's house, feeling fuller than ever before. And it wasn't just 'cause my belly was filled up with good cooking and my pockets were bulging with peanuts. It was like that big ole empty space I'd been carrying around inside me for so long got plumb filled up.

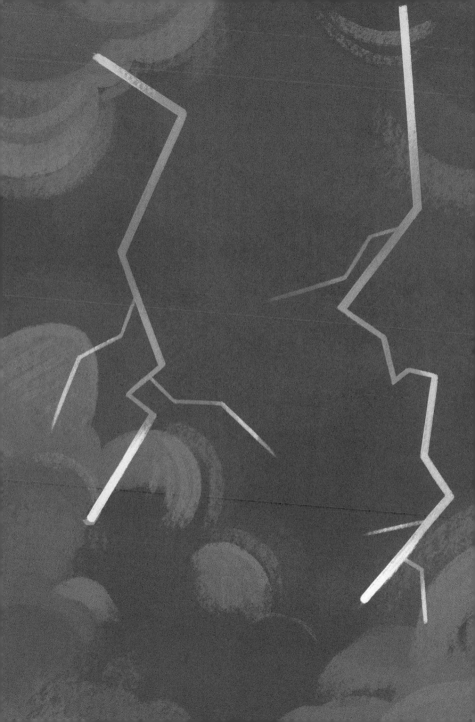

Author's Note

Years ago, I read a magazine article about a city in Spain whose Jewish community had been viciously attacked in 1391. The subject grabbed my attention. Although I knew that Jews had been expelled from Spain in 1492, the same year that Columbus sailed to the New World, I hadn't heard about the frequent attacks on Spain's Jewish communities a whole century earlier. I began reading whatever I could get my hands on about the treatment of the Jews of Spain during medieval times. Eventually, my quest led me to visit Spain and see for myself the ancient walled Jewish section of Gerona, the town featured in the magazine article.

While none of the characters in my story were real people, I based their family backgrounds on what I had learned. For example, the name *Abran de*

Gerondi, which James sees at the top of Abuela's family tree in the Bible, means that this ancestor of hers was from Gerona.

In 1391, there was a wave of anti-Jewish attacks in Spain. Historians estimate that as many as fifty thousand Jews were massacred and another one hundred thousand were forced to convert to Christianity. What caused these attacks? There is no single reason, but much of the violence was incited by Catholic religious leaders who wanted all of Spain to be Catholic. These leaders accused the Jews of being responsible for all sorts of misfortunes, including the bubonic plague, a horrible disease that caused the death of many Spanish people. Catholic leaders falsely claimed that Jews caused the plague by poisoning the water wells. Urged on by their religious leaders, Catholic peasants began demanding that the Jews accept the Christian faith or face death.

As a result, many Jews converted to Christianity, hoping to be safe from attacks and to enjoy the same rights as other Spanish citizens. They were called *conversos*, or new Christians. Conversos were forbidden from eating, drinking, visiting, or living with Jews who refused to convert. The Jews were required to dress differently from Christians too. Jewish women had to wear plain clothing that reached down to their feet and was made of coarse material. They weren't allowed to wear anything made of fine cloth. Jewish men were required to let their hair and beards grow long, and at times all the Jews had to wear red badges.

Conversos did not escape persecution either. In 1478, Queen Isabella set up an organization similar to a court, called the Inquisition, to investigate and punish converso Jews (and Muslims too) who were suspected of not being true believers in Christianity and of continuing to practice their faith in secret. Another name for the conversos was *crypto-Jews* because *crypto* means "hidden." To humiliate these secret Jews and show how unacceptable they were in Spain, people called them *Marranos*, which is Spanish for "pigs." They and their descendants were forbidden to work in certain professions, to attend college, and even to live in certain towns. To force conversos to confess to still practicing Judaism, the Inquisition used brutal methods, including torture, and took away all their property. Many conversos were put to death, often by being burned alive.

I imagine that James's ancestors would have been among those conversos who secretly continued some Jewish practices. As an example, on Friday nights, they would've honored the Jewish Sabbath by keeping their prayer books in their laps under the table and reciting the prayers while pretending to play cards. Anyone who passed by their home and looked in a window would only see that the family was playing a card game.

On March 31, 1492, King Ferdinand and Queen Isabella signed the Edict of Expulsion, which expelled all the Jews from Spain. Jews had to sell their property and leave the country within four months. Those who converted to Christianity could stay. Any Jews who failed to depart by the end of the four months faced the death penalty. On July 31, 1492, the last Jew left the soil of Spain.

Most Jews and conversos who wanted to hold on to their Jewish practices went to Portugal, North Africa, the Netherlands, and the Americas. Some Jews seeking to escape persecution joined Columbus's voyage to the New World. Columbus's translator was Jewish, the first person to sight land was a Jew, and both the ship's astronomer and the ship's doctor were Jewish.

James's ancestors also would have fled Spain at the time of the expulsion. They eventually made their way to Mexico, where James's abuela, Marlena, would've been born. At first, Jews and conversos in Mexico could semi-openly practice their faith because the region was populated with mostly non-Christian native peoples. Also, although Mexico was owned by Spain, it was far enough away to not be fully under Spanish control. But when Spain colonized the area in the late 1500s, it established the Inquisition there too. When conversos were caught observing Judaism, they were often killed.

I was surprised to learn that the Inquisition remained officially in force in Mexico until the 1800s, a time when Marlena's family would've still been living there. But I was even more surprised to discover that in Spain, the Edict of Expulsion wasn't removed from the law books until as recently as 1968! In other words, it's only been during my lifetime that Jews in Spain have been legally allowed to openly practice their religion. In 2015, the government of Spain announced that those who could prove they were descendants of the Jews expelled in 1492 can now become citizens of Spain.

For fear of being discriminated against by their Christian neighbors, most conversos have kept their Jewish ancestry hidden throughout the generations. Some crypto-Jews, like Marlena's family, migrated north from Mexico to Texas and other parts of the American Southwest. Even today, there are practicing Catholics in Texas and New Mexico who are only now discovering their Jewish roots.

I decided to set my story in Texas partly because Texas was where many crypto-Jews settled. Also, many Mexicans moved to the area in the early 1900s to build the railroad, as Marlena's family had. But of all the towns in Texas, why did I choose Odessa? The name of the city itself interested me. My maternal grandparents were Russian Jews who immigrated to the United States from another city called Odessa—in Ukraine. In my book, Paul's Russian Jewish family emigrated from Ukraine as well. Paul's father's conversion to Christianity in order to get business making Russian army uniforms is the story of my great-grandfather. There were frequent pogroms (mob attacks) against the Jews in Russia back then, so Paul's father's fate could have been my great-grandfather's fate. But nobody in my family knows what happened to him after his wife (my great-grandmother) divorced him and came to the US with her new husband.

I decided to have Paul's family settle in Odessa, Texas, mainly because its wide, flat prairies would have reminded them of their homeland. And oil was discovered in the area in the late 1920s, bringing many people there in search of jobs on the oil rigs. Certain physical features of Odessa, Texas, made it the ideal backdrop for a couple of boys having adventures. The meteor crater really exists in Odessa and is believed to be the second-largest one in the United States. Fierce sandstorms occur in the area, the terrain is dotted with buffalo wallows and mesquite, and all of the wildlife mentioned in the story—hawks, skunks, and snakes—can be found there.

Within this book, I've incorporated other aspects of my personal history as well. Pappy owns a diner because my grandfather ran a diner. And that recipe for Ridgely burgers? It came from him. I've tried to make the characters' experiences true to the time and place in which the story unfolds. In writing this book, I hope to shed some light on a part of Jewish history that has remained hidden for far too many years.

Acknowledgments

For setting me on the path to write this book, I'd like to thank Andree Aelion Brooks, the author of the article in *Reform Judaism* magazine that first sparked my interest in the Jews of Spain. My sincere gratitude goes out to the staff of PJ Our Way and its founder, Harold Grinspoon, for their generous grant award. And I'm also grateful to them, along with the Yiddish Book Center, for the opportunity to participate in the very first Tent: Children's Literature program. Kudos to the *Highlights* folks, too, for providing children's writers with stellar workshops in the most idyllic surroundings imaginable.

Thank you, as well, to the Odessa, Texas, Chamber of Commerce for their helpful responses to my inquiries and to the authors, too numerous to name, of the many resources I consulted—on Texas life in the late 1920s, on Spanish Jewry, and on the history of Russian Jews.

I owe a debt of gratitude to my family of eagle-eyed beta readers—David, Sara, and Joel—who supported me and (mostly) respected my "writer at work" glare. Many thanks, also, to my small-but-mighty writers' group—Ann Wilson and Sonya Sones—who've been the angels on my shoulder, whispering encouragement and offering invaluable critiques, lo these many years. And thanks to my agent, Karen Grencik, for helping me find a home for this book. Lastly, thank you to my dad, may his memory be a blessing, for passing on to me his love of words.

About the Author

Betsy R. Rosenthal is a writer and a former civil rights attorney. Her books include an award-winning middle grade novel in verse, *Looking for Me in this Great Big Family*; *An Ambush of Tigers*, an ALA Notable Children's Book; and *Porcupine's Picnic: Who Eats What?*. She lives in Pacific Palisades, California, with her husband and two dogs. Her three adult children are making their way in the world. To learn more, visit her at www.BetsyRosenthal.com.